"Don't look. You'll be okay." Lindsey glanced at her.

"Keep your eyes on the road." Amy couldn't tell if she had shrieked or if it just felt like it. Her head pounded and tremors coursed through her body. She closed her eyes.

"Really, Amy, maybe you should see a shrink. You're a mess."

Amy took big breaths, long and slow. She pressed her hands over her face. "Are we there yet?"

"Let's talk about something else. Tell me why you don't like the guy."

"I don't need any guys in my life right now. They cause trouble. I certainly don't have time for a guy who makes me feel miserable at every opportunity."

"I thought it made perfect sense to distract you," Lindsey said. "If you identify your fears and confront them, they won't bother you."

"Really?" Amy peered between her fingers. "What do you think about spiders?"

"Spiders are different. They can kill you. They creep around and spin sticky webs. No thanks. Spiders are scary."

"So are strange guys." Amy squeezed her eyes shut again.

MICHELLE ULE

Navy wife Michelle Ule is a writer, genealogist, and Bible study leader. She graduated from UCLA with a degree in English Literature and married a submarine officer whom she followed all over the world with their four children. Michelle lives in northern California with her family.

Bridging Two Hearts

Michelle Ule

Heartsong Presents

For Robert,
My favorite navy guy
And
With admiration and respect for
the women and their families who love
Navy SEALs

A note from the Author:

*I love to hear from my readers! You may correspond with me
by writing:*

**Michelle Ule
Author Relations
P.O. Box 9048
Buffalo, NY 14240-9048**

ISBN-13: 978-0-373-48645-8

BRIDGING TWO HEARTS

This edition issued by special arrangement with Barbour Publishing,
Inc., 1810 Barbour Drive, Uhrichsville, Ohio, U.S.A.

Scripture taken from the Holy Bible, New International Version®.
NIV®. Copyright © 1973, 1978, 1984, 2011 by Biblica, Inc.™ Used by
permission. All rights reserved worldwide.

This is a work of fiction. Names, characters, places and incidents are
either the product of the author's imagination or are used fictitiously,
and any resemblance to actual persons, living or dead, business
establishments, events or locales is entirely coincidental.

Chapter 1

Of course Josh Murphy saw the girl as soon as he climbed on the airport bus. Who could miss a babe like her? Big brown eyes, honey blond hair, cute little figure; but what caught his attention was her hands. They shook despite the death grip on the seat in front of her.

Was this a damsel in distress, or what?

Pete nudged him in the back with a green duffel bag. "Hey, Doc, get on board."

"Right." Josh eased his bag down the aisle and took a seat in front of the girl. Pete and Flip flung their duffels on the other side of the bus and sat down.

The bus door slid shut with a hiss, locking out the salty ocean air. "You sailors going to NAB?" the bus driver asked as he checked his mirror and pulled onto the highway in front of San Diego's Lindbergh Field Airport.

His teammates turned to Josh.

"Yeah, take us to the Naval Amphibious Base. We need to check in."

The bus driver shook his head. "Good luck. You guys need it in your job."

Josh grinned as he looked out the window at the palm trees lining the blue sun-kissed bay. San Diego sparkled in the June morning. He felt relieved to be out of the Gulf Coast's muggy air and thankful to be alive after the tight spot his team had been in. He glanced across the aisle. Flip had tugged his ball cap over his face and leaned back as if to nap.

"Hiya, Princess." Pete noticed the girl sitting behind Josh.

"Hi," she said, her shoulders rigid and face tense. "I don't usually talk to strangers."

"We're not strangers; we're America's saviors."

"You can't save me from this one." Her lower lip trembled.

"Hey, Doc, tell her what we are." Pete flexed his generous biceps.

"Doc?" Her chin rose and her face brightened. "Are you a doctor?"

"I'm a navy corpsman. My name's Josh. Are *you* a doctor?"

She clenched her trembling hands into her lap. "I'm Amy. And no, I'm not a doctor, I'm a massage therapist hoping to become a physical therapist. I like to ease people's pain."

Just looking at her was helping him. "It's satisfying to see someone get better, isn't it?"

"Absolutely. People come in hurting and after one hour with me they're relaxed and happy. I love my job."

Pete rolled his shoulders and rotated his neck. "I've been sitting on a plane all night, I could use some muscle rubbing."

She showed the shadow of a pixie smile. "My job's a little more sophisticated than that."

"Where do you work?" Josh stretched his arm across the rough plastic back of his seat.

"I've been at San Diego State's athletic center, but I just started working over there." She jerked her head to the right.

Josh saw the busy harbor full of military and luxury boats, the curving flat bridge and the Coronado shoreline. "On the island?"

"At the Hotel Del Coronado. I can hardly believe it."

"That's where we're headed," Pete said. "Home to Coronado."

Josh ignored him. "What can't you believe?"

"I got a job at the Del. It's one of the fanciest resorts in America. Did you ever see the old movie *Some Like It Hot*?"

"With Jack Lemmon and Marilyn Monroe? Sure. Hilarious."

"It took place at the Del. I'm thrilled to work there."

"So, what's the problem?"

She swallowed so hard it felt painful to watch. "The bridge."

He shrugged. "So?"

"Doesn't anything scare you?"

Pete laughed. "No. We like people to be afraid of us."

Amy stared. "I don't understand."

Pete thrust out his chest. "We blow things up, like James Bond."

"Really?" she squeaked.

Josh scowled at his roommate. "Only to defend our country from the bad guys."

Amy frowned. "So in addition to being afraid of the bridge, I should be afraid of you?"

The bus stopped to admit three teenage boys with boogie boards and two plump women dressed in white uniforms.

Josh focused on the boogie boards. "How have the waves been this week on Coronado?"

"I don't know about the waves, but the beach in front of the Del is terrific."

The bridge loomed as they passed Petco Park. Josh wondered if the Padres were in town. "You like baseball?"

Amy stared at the on-ramp.

Josh rapped on the window beside her head. "Don't look at it. It's just a roadway over water, no big deal. It doesn't even have towers. Relax"

"You don't understand." Her voice sounded shaky. "I prayed about the ride, but I'm still terrified."

Pete punched his arm. "Hey, Doc, help the lady out. Get on your knees and pray."

"There's nothing to worry about." Josh put humor in his voice. "We're trained divers. If the bus falls off the bridge, we'll save you."

"You're not the slightest bit funny. You don't understand at all." She shuddered.

How could anyone be so frightened by a mere road? Sure, it went high in the air, but the bus wouldn't fall off. What was her problem? "Listen, if you're a praying woman, it shouldn't matter what happens. If you get to the other side, great; if you die, you get to be with Jesus. I call that a win-win."

Was a tear slipping out of her clamped-shut eyes?

"I love this view," Pete said.

Amy whimpered.

Josh couldn't control his hand any more than he had his words. He touched her arm. "It's going to be okay." Warmth suddenly ran through his chest.

She opened her eyes. "What did you do?"

Josh put up his hands in surrender. "Nothing."

"Did you feel something when you touched me?" She leaned forward.

"I apologize. I shouldn't have touched your arm without asking. But look. You're over the bridge."

She slumped against the seat and turned her head away. As the bus rode down Orange Avenue's business district, Josh tried to think of something to wipe away her misery. When they reached her stop at the entrance to the 1887 white Victorian hotel, she brushed past the men, head down. But when she got to the front she paused and stared back at Josh, one long appealing look that tore at his heart.

And then she got off the bus.

Chapter 2

Sprawled along the beach, the Hotel Del Coronado dominated the landscape. Even as Amy turned her back on the terrifying bridge and the rowdy sailors on the bus, she felt her heart soar with expectation. This job could make the difference in so many ways. She could hardly wait to get to work.

Located at the end of Orange Avenue where it turned into Silver Strand Boulevard, the hotel served as both the linchpin and the focal point for many local activities. Four stories high and built of wood, it featured a red, cone-shaped roof on the southern end atop which flew an American flag.

Amy entered on the north side of the building through a door reserved for employees. She walked down a cement-floored corridor lined with overhead plumbing and electrical lines. Pushing through a white door, she entered the spa's warren of rooms, and the atmosphere turned tranquil, plush, and perfumed.

A colleague her age, Jackie, greeted her in the break room. "How was your bus ride?"

"I survived." Amy set her black backpack into a metal locker and tugged her mint-green uniform into place. She paused at the mirror beside the door and centered her name-tag properly above the spa logo.

"Perfect," Jackie said. "Let's check today's appointments at the front desk."

A reed-thin middle-aged woman with a severe haircut, Kathy, supervised the therapists. "We'll start you easy on your first day. You've got two Swedish massages interspersed with manning the front desk. You'll probably have more clients this afternoon. Okay?"

"Yes."

Kathy crossed her arms. "I'm curious about the audition massage. How did you know the housekeeper had a bum knee?"

Amy thought before answering. Could she tell her supervisor she had prayed first? "Housekeeping is a hard job," she finally said. "Knees take a lot of punishment."

"That massage got you the job. Keep finding sweet spots, and you'll do well here. Let me show you around. You seemed a little frazzled last week at your orientation."

Amy nodded. Her attempt to drive over the bridge that day had been a disaster. Anxiety about the commute had made it difficult to concentrate during her orientation—hence her decision to take the bus that morning.

"The bridge makes me nervous," she said.

Kathy laughed. "You'll need to get over it if you're going to work here."

Amy agreed and went for her first client.

The heavy middle-aged woman gushed as she entered the dimmed room. "I feel better already. The soft music, the candles, the fragrances, it must be heaven to spend the entire day here."

Amy left the room while the woman removed her robe and got settled under the warmed sheet on the massage table. When she returned, Amy prayed for wisdom and then rubbed warmed oil onto her hands. She folded back the sheet and pushed long gentle strokes from the woman's lower back into her shoulders.

Amy could feel the woman's tense muscles as she slid her hands along the upper spine. Slow and steady, Amy worked in silence, paying close attention to the client. She pushed down with more firmness until the tough muscles softened and the woman sighed.

"It's satisfying to see someone get better." Amy's mind replayed the sailor's tenor voice and something inside her hummed. But then she remembered how callously he had treated her fear.

"There's a sore spot," the woman murmured.

Amy picked up her hands in surprise and then had to reclaim her focus. She circled through the woman's upper back with her middle fingers, pushing against the resistance and feeling the flesh warm.

The warmth reminded her of that navy guy's touch and how something seemed to spark. She was used to getting a sense about the people she massaged, but had never felt anything like that before. Amy racked her brain trying to remember what other therapists had said about an unexpected flash—or whatever it was.

Amy shook her head. It must have been a fluke.

"Have you been doing this long?"

Amy modulated her voice to a croon. "Four years."

"Your husband must love you."

She'd heard that before and had a standard answer. "I'm sure he will someday."

Jackie joined her at break time. "Let's get away from all the aromatherapy." They grabbed their lunches and headed outside to a bench facing the ocean.

Amy watched the surf roll in, the foam whiter than she expected. Children in colorful suits frolicked in the shallows, and intrepid middle schoolers ran into the waves with yellow boogie boards. The breeze felt delightful in the warm sun as Amy bit into her peanut butter and jelly sandwich.

When they finished eating, Jackie suggested a walk.

They strolled along the shorefront all the way to the south end of the hotel property, stopping at PeDel's Bike Rentals. Jackie checked her watch. "This is the ten-minute mark. I'd love to walk down to the beach where the SEALs train, but we can't bring sand back into the spa."

"SEALs train at the Hotel Del's beach?"

Jackie sighed. "They go by here all the time, you'll see them. I love to watch those handsome hunks run up the beach in their wet suits. It's one of the perks of this job."

"I'll look forward to that," Amy said.

The rest of the afternoon went well. Amy returned to the bus stop at six-thirty, tired but thrilled with the forty dollars in tips she had earned. She smiled her thanks to God in heaven and then noticed thin clouds moving to the east in the direction of the bridge. Her confidence faltered as doom threatened.

Two men wearing brown shirts and black shorts ran up the street in her direction. Amy blinked twice when the tanned guy with blue-black hair in the lead picked up the pace and ran toward her, a wide grin spread across his face.

"Hey, Amy, that you?" Josh couldn't believe it. He'd thought about her all day long, even as he debriefed at his duty station a mile down Silver Strand Boulevard.

"Sure looks like her, Doc." Pete matched Josh's long legs stride for stride. "But she doesn't look very happy to see you."

They jogged to a stop beside the young woman. "How'd your day go?" Josh asked.

"Good. It's a great place to work." Amy clutched her back-pack to her chest.

Pete put his hands on his hips and bent toward the ground

panting while Josh scrutinized the complex to their left. "Where do you work in the Del?"

"I work at the spa over on the water side."

Josh filled his lungs with the cleansing ocean air. "That's right. Massage therapy. Have any interesting clients?"

She blinked. "I don't discuss my clients."

"Right. Anything unusual happen?" Just looking at her pretty face was making things happen inside him.

Amy shrugged. "A normal workday. How about you?"

"Same. Hurry up, wait, that's the navy way. Training starts tomorrow."

"It'll be fun," Pete said. "Mud, sleep deprivation, ocean swimming, sand, fleas, and eating raw fish. Just like summer camp."

Her eyes widened. "Really?"

Josh snickered. "That's the trainees, not us. We're lucky to be past BUD/S."

Pete poked him. "I thought you didn't believe in luck."

"I don't." Josh felt almost light-headed as he looked at Amy. "We're blessed in this job."

"Blessed?" She sounded puzzled.

"Yeah, blessed. We serve our country, protect damsels like you, and get a good workout. It's a great job. Don't you believe me?"

A surprised smile broke through. "I think I do."

"Good. Where're you headed now?"

The smile fled. "Home?"

"You don't sound like you mean it."

She looked to the northeast. Josh only saw the downtown shops along Orange Avenue and the spire of his church.

"I have to go over the bridge," Amy whispered.

"You got over it this morning and survived. What's the big deal?"

Her face shut down. "You don't get it, do you?"

"You need me to pray again?"

The bus stopped with grinding brakes. "Good luck with your job," she said to Pete. As she stepped onto the bus, she turned toward Josh, made a face and stuck out her tongue.

"I'm sorry," Josh called.

Pete elbowed him. "Smooth. Let's go."

The bus headed north with Pete jogging after it in the direction of their apartment while Josh wondered, for the millionth time, why he always said the wrong thing.

Chapter 3

Summertime brought tourists in great numbers to the beaches and cultural events on Coronado Island across the bay from downtown San Diego. With all the visitors, traffic moved slowly along clogged streets even on a Thursday evening.

Amy watched the scenery as the bus rumbled down Orange Avenue. They passed art galleries, boutiques, and restaurants. Lamb's Players Theatre took up part of a block, and across the street, athletic men wearing brown T-shirts hoisted glasses of amber liquid in an outdoor patio. A long line waited outside the new movie theater. Couples walked dogs and babies while runners dodged them all.

"Hurry or we'll be late for the game," an older teenage boy wearing a ball cap called to the bus driver. He nudged the girl with a pierced eyebrow sitting beside him.

Amy glanced at the kid and noticed the girl had a mitt on her lap. Amy hadn't been to a baseball game in years. That nosey Josh had asked if she liked baseball. She hardly knew. Amy had worked on baseball players at San Diego

State; pitchers always needed their shoulders massaged. She'd liked them.

Where would she be going on a summer night in early June if she didn't have to worry about paying the rent or getting up for work the next morning? Amy bent her elbow on the windowsill and leaned her forehead on her hand.

"Wow, those guys run fast," the pierced girl said. "That black guy's sure buff."

The boy leaned over her. "You don't want to meet one of those guys in a dark place." He peered out the window. "You think they're racing us to the bridge?"

"They'll get there first with this traffic."

"Relax," Amy whispered. She closed her eyes and took deep cleansing breaths. "Breathe in, breathe out. Don't think about the bridge."

Immediately, an image of the high flat bridge with a hook toward downtown shoved into her mind. Amy caught her breath and felt the muscles in her tired arms contract, even as her palms grew slippery with sweat.

She willed herself to take another deep breath, pushing out her diaphragm so far the air filled her lungs practically to her stomach. She released the air slowly, blowing through slightly parted lips. Amy dropped her shoulders and let her head fall limp to her chest. She opened her fists and let her hands sag.

"They're crossing the street and hailing the bus," said the girl.

"Here's the turn to the bridge!" shouted the boy.

"I love how it looks all lit up at night." The girl pointed up. "It reminds me of a ribbon of light flying to the solar system."

The boy laughed. "It's high."

"I like it. It feels like you're sailing through thin air."

Amy whimpered and gathered her backpack to her stomach, curling around it as best she could in the bus seat. Her heart beat so fast it hurt and her throat felt blocked. She squeezed her eyes shut and a soft tear slipped out.

Rocking slowly, she whispered the one verse that helped.

"What's with you?" The boy's words ripped in her direction.

" 'Even though I walk through the darkest valley, I will fear no evil, for you are with me.' "

"We're not going through a valley, we're crossing a bridge."

Amy whispered the words again as she felt the bus hiss to a stop. The bus doors opened, bringing in the cooling night air. "You guys going my way?" the bus driver boomed.

"We need to board for a minute, sir. My friend will take care of everything. You got any money, Pete?"

"Make it fast or pay the fare." The driver laughed. "You're not going to try anything funny are you?"

"Of course not, we're checking on our friend," Pete said.

"You guys have ninety seconds until the light changes, and then I'm throwing you off. I've got a schedule to keep."

"It shouldn't take long, sir."

Was this a nightmare? Amy lifted her head and saw Josh, his sweaty shirt sticking to his chest, making his way down the aisle toward her. "What are you doing here?"

"You okay, Amy? We were running by and you looked upset. We thought we'd check on you."

She could smell his sweat and her stomach turned over. "Are you stalking me? Leave me alone. I don't need cruel people in my life."

"Cruel?" His voice rose. "We ran down this bus to make sure you're okay, and now you say I'm cruel?"

He had a point. She hated being rude. "I'll be fine."

"I prayed for you as the bus drove off, and then something made me think I should double-check. Do you need us to cross with you so you can feel safe?"

"I'm perfectly safe on the bus. Go save another part of America," Amy snapped.

"Time to go," Pete said.

"Good luck and I mean it," Josh said.

"I thought you didn't believe in luck."

"I don't. Good night." He tugged at the cord and the bus door opened. The two men jumped off.

Amy puffed out her cheeks and watched them go. It almost felt good to be so angry.

"Smooth," Pete said. "You going to patent that method of getting a girl's attention?"

Josh grinned. "Did you see how mad she was?"

"Yeah. Aren't you the one who tells me to get along with others?"

"Shake your fist at the bus."

Amy glared back at them.

"That should do the trick."

Pete shook his head. "She's riled with you."

"She's so mad, she won't think about the bridge until she's on the other side."

Pete's slow smile showed bright white teeth against his dark skin. "Brilliant, but your words are going to get you in real trouble someday. You better be careful."

"You always say that." Josh looked both ways before jogging across the street. "I'm headed to the firehouse to see Carlos. You coming?"

"Nah, your buddy cooks a mean steak, but I'm going to have a drink with the rest of the team at McP's. I'll see you at home."

"You'll live cleaner if you visit Carlos."

"Clean living's your deal. I like to fit in with the guys."

Pete turned at the corner while Josh ran down Orange Avenue's grass median. He turned right onto Sixth Street and loped to the back door of the firehouse, where he followed his nose to Carlos Sanchez, overseeing the grill.

"Captain America returns," Carlos said as he reached for the squirt bottle. "Is the world still safe for democracy?"

"I believe so. Any good fires while I was gone?" Josh savored the scent of roasting tri-tip.

"The best one's right here. Did you come for dinner?"

"I won't say no."

"It'll cost you a story. Where've you been?"

"I'd hate to have to kill you before the meat's done," Josh said. "Training."

Carlos eyed him. "Any blood?"

"Pete got nipped by a crab, but I took care of it. It got a bit dicey in a narrow spot, but we escaped. I prefer San Diego's weather."

"You and the rest of the world. What do you mean dicey?"

Josh made his face go blank and looked back at his friend.

"Is this one of those 'need-to-know situations'?"

Josh remained silent.

"I get the nonmessage." Carlos turned the sizzling meat in a cloud of smoke. "The neighbors love it when we barbeque. Where is Pete?"

"Off with the guys. He sends his love."

"I'll bet. Bible study starts tomorrow night, book of James. You on?"

Josh shrugged. "Probably. Any new women at the study?"

"College girls and summer help."

Amy's frightened eyes and trembling hands popped into Josh's mind. Maybe a Bible study could help her fear. "Don't you think college girls are starting to look young?"

The firefighter punched Josh's hard bicep. "You turning into an old man at twenty-six?"

"Maybe. You know anything about fear of bridges?" Josh asked. "I met a good looker today who's terrified of the bridge."

"Lots of people are afraid of bridges. CHP had a basket case recently. Some woman totally freaked out on the San Diego side, nearly drove off the bridge. They found her shivering in the driver's seat but desperate to get over for a job interview. One of the officers drove the kid to work. They told her to take Silver Strand Boulevard south and go home via Imperial Beach."

"What did she look like?"

Carlos grabbed the platter and moved a perfectly roasted piece of meat onto it. "How should I know? They told us the story over coffee."

"Why would anyone afraid of a bridge take a job in Coronado?"

Carlos rubbed his fingers together. "Money. You remember—the root of all evil."

"Only when you love it." Josh cracked his knuckles. "I'll pass on dinner. You think Pastor Wayne's home?"

"I saw them walk by with the kids and the dog half an hour ago."

Josh shook Carlos's hand and walked back to the street. An idea was forming in his head, and he needed to share it. If he hurried, he could catch the Poppins family before they settled in for the night.

Chapter 4

"You made it!" Lindsey crowed. "I knew you could manage the bus. How did it go?"

Amy dumped her backpack on the floor and flopped onto the couch. It had taken her ninety minutes to ride the bus home from Coronado, and she was exhausted. "What's for dinner?"

Her roommate opened the refrigerator. "Leftover takeout from last night. Salad. I could brew up noodles."

Amy rubbed her eyes and smelled the remnants of sea spray lotion on her fingertips. She craved protein.

"Any meat?"

She heard a refrigerator drawer being opened and shut. "Lunch meat. We've got cheddar cheese and yogurt." Lindsey looked at her around the door. "There might be tuna in the cupboard. I could mix it with noodles."

When had she last eaten her mother's pot roast? Amy's mouth watered at the memory of a good piece of meat with mashed potatoes and gravy. Low-fat yogurt wouldn't fill the need, and she was too tired and broke to go to the grocery store.

"Any frozen peas so I can have the full tuna casserole treatment?"

"Coming right up."

As Lindsey filled a pot with water, Amy closed her eyes and thought about the day. Other than the commute, she'd enjoyed it. She'd learned new ways to use her forearms to work out knots in clients' backs. Her colleagues had been friendly and helpful, like most massage therapists she knew. A very good day.

"Ethan came by looking for you."

Amy frowned. "Ethan from my psych class? What did he want?"

"A date."

The tone in Lindsey's voice made Amy look up. "What?"

"He's an operator. Be careful with him. Does he have your phone number?"

"No." She had no idea what Ethan wanted from her, and she didn't want to find out. "He's a case of no good deed goes unpunished. I wish I'd never shared my lecture notes with him."

Maybe she could avoid him by disappearing to Coronado. If she could get there.

"Did you have any problems with the bridge?" Lindsey drained the tuna and dumped it in a bowl.

The bridge. Amy's stomach tightened. She didn't want to think about the bridge.

"Ames?"

"I got over it."

"Great. Was it as bad as you feared?

Amy plucked at a stray thread on her shirt. "It's worse. Some navy guys gave me a hard time going over and then made me so mad coming home, I couldn't even think straight."

"You met some sailors?" Lindsey perched on the rounded arm of the couch. "What were they like?"

"Josh has a loud mouth and thinks he knows everything. His buddy Pete was proud of how strong he is. Ridiculous."

"Cute?"

Cute? Josh's vivid blue eyes twinkled when he spoke to her, sure, and his ebony hair, while short, shone. Should a sailor have such beautiful hair?

"Amy?"

"Pete's got the smooth dark brown skin some black guys get. He shaves his head. Josh has spent a lot of time in the sun."

"Tall, short, fat, skinny? I need details."

Amy stretched her legs. "They were both really buff. They looked like they work out all the time, and they were good runners."

"Runners? On the bus?"

Amy explained about the encounters. "Josh made me so mad. He said all these awful things and made fun of me. I don't know why I listened to him."

The noodle water boiled over with a hiss. Lindsey dumped in the noodles and stirred the pot with a long wooden spoon. "Tell me more while I put this together."

Amy hated tuna casserole, a dish her mother had made too many times to count in her childhood, but it was cheap and filling. Anytime the paychecks got thin, Amy knew what they'd be having for dinner, even if her mother tried to dress it up with odd food corralled from food pantries around town.

"So, this Pete was dark, was he tall and handsome, too?"

She vaguely recalled a bright smile and a rich tenor voice. Josh's surprising touch and challenging words had caught her attention. Had she misunderstood? Didn't he say he was a praying guy? Why was he so obnoxious?

Lindsey opened a can of cream of mushroom soup. "Are you okay?"

"Tired. They were both good looking. Pete's probably six feet tall, Josh only a couple inches taller than me, maybe five

foot ten. It doesn't really matter. I'll never see them again."
Amy frowned. "They did distract me, though, which made
it easier to cross the bridge. That bridge is my real problem.
I don't know if I can do it again."

Lindsey set down the can and reached for her laptop. "I've
got good news. I found another way to get to Coronado." As
she logged on she bit her lower lip. "I don't know about the
price, but at least you won't have to take the bridge."

Amy roused herself to look over her roommate's shoulder
at a colorful web page. "The ferry?"

"It's not a bridge. You're not afraid of water are you?"

Wayne Poppins, a lean man in his midthirties leaned
against the white picket fence in front of his house with the
easy grace of a longtime golfer. He crossed his arms as Josh
approached. "How long are you back for?"

Josh appreciated that his pastor understood about his job
and didn't give him a hard time. One of his former teammates
had stopped going to church after his pastor razzed him too
often about missed Sundays and vagueness when answering
work questions.

"I'm home for a while."

Pastor Wayne nodded. "Anything else you can tell me?"

"I'm happy to be back, we had a successful trip, and we'll
be leaving eventually."

"Don't get married as long as you're with this outfit. Your
comings and goings would drive a woman crazy." Pastor
Wayne nodded at his wife coming out the front door carrying a sleek calico cat.

"I'm not sure I want to hug you, Josh. You're all sweaty."
Darlin set the cat down and patted his arm. "Your muscles
are like stone."

"I work hard to stay this strong." Josh laughed. "How are
the kids?"

"Safely in bed. Are you coming to the Bible study tomorrow night? I'll make your favorite cookies."

"Yes, ma'am. I'll be there."

"I'll pray Pete comes, too. I've been on my knees for him."

"Thanks."

"Is this a social call?" Pastor Wayne pulled an optimistic weed from a crack in the sidewalk. He stood up abruptly. "Has something happened?"

"I met a woman on the bus today who's afraid of the bridge." Josh thumbed over his shoulder in the direction of the fire station. "Carlos tells me it's a common problem, and I wondered if she'd be better off living on the island rather than having to cross the bridge every day to work." He knelt to scratch the purring cat's chin.

When Josh didn't say anything more, Pastor Wayne cleared his throat and scuffed at the sidewalk with his loafers. "Who is this woman?"

"Her name's Amy, and she's a massage therapist at the Del. I wondered if anyone at church has an extra room to rent."

"Is she looking for a place to live? Who is she?"

Who was she? A pretty girl afraid of a bridge who worked at the local spa, whose fear had been so palpable it got through his emotional defenses, not to mention made his blood feel hot? She had big eyes and perfect lips and a spunky spirit he didn't see often. Of course how many nice girls did he meet at his job?

"When I touched her, there was this spark."

Darlin's eyebrows disappeared into her brilliant blond bangs. "When you touched her? Give us more details. This sounds romantic."

"It wasn't romantic." At least he didn't think so. "My job depends on intuition. I've got to know when to react and when not to react. It makes you a shrewd judge of people, and you make decisions fast. That's all I'm saying. She had a cross around her neck, and she prays. I figured she was one of us and needed help. So I helped her."

Wayne Poppins laughed when Josh outlined the day's encounters.

"I might know someone, but we'll need to learn more about Amy," Darlin said. "Bring her to Bible study tomorrow night."

"I thought you wanted me to bring Pete? I don't know if I'll ever see her again."

"Find out more about her," Pastor Wayne said. "For all you know, she doesn't need help."

Josh didn't agree but figured he'd better think about it some more. Jumping to conclusions wasn't part of his job description. He ran his hand along the back of his neck and said good night.

A cool breeze blew up from the Pacific Ocean less than a mile away. Tendrils of fog drifted between the mixture of old wooden cottages and new modern condos that filled the town. Josh stopped to salute the late Admiral Stockdale's home, where the widow of the highest-ranking POW from Vietnam still lived. He liked to acknowledge the good guys.

Summer darkness had fallen, and the pale golden streetlights lit only portions of the sidewalk. From habit, he fell into the shadows and slipped along quietly. He surprised more than one dog owner—though never their leashed dogs—and came up on catlike feet to a 1950s adobe home. A light burned in the small apartment above the garage as Josh turned down the narrow path to the side gate.

He grinned and grabbed the top of the wall. He liked to practice commando tricks when possible, so with a fluid motion he pulled himself up and over the top. He landed on the balls of his feet beside the trash can.

A motion-detection light flashed on, and Josh heard a gruff voice. "I've got a gun, and you're in trouble, mister."

Chapter 5

"I'll see you at the Del at two o'clock," Lindsey said as she dropped off Amy at the dock. "I'm going to take advantage of the elegant spa experience today."

Amy watched her roommate pull into traffic on downtown San Diego's main thoroughfare and then turned toward Broadway Pier.

She hoped the ferry would give her another alternative to get to work, but peering at the listed parking fees in the nearby lots, Amy knew she probably couldn't afford this commute plan either. But it would be fun to ride a boat, even at seven o'clock in the morning. The walk from the ferry terminal to the hotel on the other side of the island, a straight mile and a half down Orange Avenue, would be a terrific way to start the workday.

"A grand morning for a cruise," said the elderly man in the ticket booth. "Going to work?"

"Yes, at the hotel Del."

He held out a blue ticket. "Commuters travel free on the seven twenty ferry."

"What about the return?"

"If you travel during the commute hours, we'll give you a free commuter pass back."

Flutters of hope stirred. "Really?"

"Yes." He pointed to the end of the pier. "The Silvergate will be here soon."

"Thank you, Lord," she whispered.

Amy adjusted her backpack as she joined other commuters standing by the landing. The product used at the Hotel Del was superior to what she was used to, her skin felt delicious and smooth in the fresh morning air. Even after a shower and a night home, when she put her hands to her nose she could smell the sweetness of the rich massage oil. Knowing she was part of such a luxurious spa setting made her feel as confident and secure as the clientele she served.

That afternoon, Amy had permission to practice her new Hotel Del methods on her roommate. Happy to spend her day off getting a massage and relaxing in the Del's spa, Lindsey volunteered to take Amy to dinner in Coronado afterward and then give her a ride home.

The jaunty little Silvergate ferry, blue on the bottom and white on top, arrived with a high toot. After the Coronado commuters exited, Amy and a dozen others boarded and climbed the stairs to sit on the upper deck.

From her perch, Amy observed San Diego's busy waterfront. A cruise liner filled the next pier and farther down a World War II aircraft carrier awaited tourists later in the day. The metal and glass skyscrapers of downtown San Diego gleamed in the early-morning light. As the little ferry started across the bay, Amy could see the flatlands of the North Island Navy Base on Coronado Island. Two navy ships were moored on the bay side, not far from a line of waterfront houses and hotels.

The caw of seagulls soaring above and the salty scent of the sea made her smile. Way off to the west Point Loma reached toward the narrow entrance of San Diego bay. As the ferry turned south, Amy could see the line of cars sprinting across the white cement Coronado Bridge. If only she could conquer her fear and drive, the commute would be simple. But even as she looked up, she trembled. Bad things happened on bridges.

Taking the ferry every day would be complicated—she'd either have to ride the bus from home or park at ten dollars a day. The ferry could solve her commute problems, but it would be a whole lot easier and faster if she conquered the bridge.

Amy rummaged through her backpack's side pocket for the green Gideon's New Testament. Just slightly larger than her palm, it had scripture suggestions for life's problems listed on the front pages. Amy looked up courage: Psalm 27:14. It would be her verse for the day: "Wait for the Lord; be strong and take heart and wait for the Lord."

"Wait for what?" she whispered. "A solution to my commute problem? Will You strengthen my heart from worrying about the bridge?"

A gull landed on the railing beside her and cocked its head, staring at her with a yellow eye circled in orange. "I'm not afraid of you." Amy laughed.

The ferry turned toward the Coronado landing. Off to the right, Amy watched sailors working on the navy ships. At the end of the navy base, estates crowded the shore facing the San Diego skyline. A cluster of greenery indicated a small park where two men wearing brown shirts carried an orange kayak toward the water.

As the ferry neared the wooden landing jutting out into the bay, Amy looked up at the bridge and laughed. It hadn't defeated her commute that day. Now she merely had to walk a mile and a half to work on a splendid June morning. She could hardly wait to get started.

* * *

"How long did old man Calloway keep you last night?" Pete adjusted his end of the kayak as they reached the water.

"About an hour. Mrs. Calloway had gone to bed early, and he was lonely. They surprised me with the motion detector, though. I'd have come through the gate differently if I'd known the lights would go on."

"You're slipping, Doc. You should have done a better reconnoiter."

Josh agreed. "Danger comes when you least expect it. Home turf can be the worst."

"I talked to both of them when I got back," Pete said. "They'd set aside the mail in a box. He told me a couple sea stories, asked for two in return and let me go. They wanted to watch *Wheel of Fortune*."

"If only the movie makers knew how glamorous the life of a Navy SEAL really is," Josh said.

"They'd laugh us out of the fleet."

Josh felt terrific after eight hours of sleep in his own bed and now the expectation of a paddle down the bay side of Coronado to NAB—the Naval Amphibious Base—in lieu of PT. Chief was not usually so generous, but maybe he'd decided to have mercy on them after a tough couple of days.

They'd carried the two-man kayak three blocks from their apartment to Bay View Park, a tiny opening between waterfront houses. Once there, they skirted purple agapanthus on a twisted path leading to the water.

Wearing his sports sandals, Pete walked into the bay and floated the kayak. Josh secured their gear and followed him in. Pete nodded and they pushed off from shore, headed to the right where they'd watch the little Coronado ferry berth at the landing and then continue past.

"All those happy tourists coming over to play," Pete said as they floated out of the boat lane. The Silvergate darted through the water, throwing up a minor wake. They could smell the diesel smoke.

Josh glanced at his waterproof watch. "It's early for tourists. Those are probably folks coming to work."

"Hey!" Pete put up his paddle in greeting. "There's your friend off the bus."

Josh looked up to the top deck, and there she was, the fearful Amy. He waved but she did not respond. The Silvergate blew its whistle three times and stopped at the dock.

"I understand she might be angry at you," Pete said. "But why won't she wave at me?"

"We've got a couple minutes, let's go ask her."

Pete turned around and gave him a hard look. "No. We need to go to work. Besides she's running away."

Josh watched Amy scamper onto the pier as soon as the ship tied up. She scurried toward the shopping area at the top of the landing without looking back. "We'd never catch her, even if we didn't have the kayak."

Pete laughed. "We could catch her, easy. But what's the fascination? You only met her twice."

"She seems like a lost soul."

"And you want to save her? Don't bother. We won't be around long enough." He splashed water in Josh's direction. "Let's go."

Josh hit the timer on his watch and they stroked wide around the ferry landing lanes. He and Pete swung the two-bladed paddles with a familiar rhythm and kayaked around the corner to Tidelands Park. They slalomed between moored sailboats near the bridge. Pete pointed at the sign warning them to keep their speed under five miles per hour. "No problem."

Josh flipped bay water at Pete. He could hear the rattle of commuter cars on the bridge as the kayak slipped under the concrete roadway into shadow. A little farther down, early-morning golfers dotted the verdant golf course. He could smell the fresh-mown grass.

They paddled in sync for ten minutes before cutting across Glorietta Bay to the NAB. Halfway across, a small shore patrol boat intercepted them. Pete pulled the military ID from his breast pocket and held it aloft.

"Where are you headed?" a voice called through a bullhorn.

"SEAL team three."

"We'll follow you in and check you out."

Pete and Josh saluted and pulled into the dock where an MP awaited. "Who do you work for?"

"Chief Rossi," Josh replied as he shipped his paddle.

"You must be Smith and Murphy."

"Aye-aye."

"I still need to see your IDs."

They handed them over, climbed out of the kayak and waited for the ID check before pocketing their cards. They lifted the wet boat onto their shoulders and stowed it away before finishing their commute to work by crossing the street.

Some days were just like that.

Easy.

Chapter 6

"You've got a newbie first thing." Jackie pointed at the computerized appointment calendar.

"How do you know she's new?" Amy straightened the lotion bottles, pausing to sniff a citrus oil.

"I took the phone call this morning, and the woman burbled about how it was her first visit and she needed a young woman plus extra consideration for her nervousness."

Amy shrugged. "Why didn't you take her?"

"I was already booked. It's a fifty-minute massage. Be gentle."

Amy laughed. "No problem."

"Darlin Poppins," the petite thirty-something client said when Amy shook her cool hand at eleven forty-five. "I know it's a silly name, but I can't help who my parents were or who I fell in love with. So I'm stuck with it."

"Darlin?"

"Short for darling. My father's idea."

Amy froze before she thought of an answer. "Your dad sounds like a clever man who knows women."

"Yes. How about yours?"

"Not so good."

Amy led her through the cream-colored door to the dressing room. She hung a white cotton robe on the hook in a cubicle and showed Darlin Poppins where to lock up her possessions. Amy had to demonstrate the locker key system several times before Darlin could focus long enough to work it herself.

"I've never had a massage before," Darlin said for the third time. "I'm so nervous. What do I do now?"

"Take off your clothes, lock them up, and then I'll get you settled in the relaxation room for a cup of tea or sparkling water before we begin." Amy modulated her voice and spoke quietly and slowly. "This is an oasis out of time for you to enjoy and feel pampered."

Darlin brightened. "You're absolutely right. Mrs. Martin said I need to relax and let you pamper me. I don't have to do a thing, just relax, be quiet, and sit by the pool. I brought a book to read. Heavenly."

"Who is Mrs. Martin?"

"The admiral's widow. You've heard of Admiral Hiram Martin? She goes to our church and has a monthly massage here. She gave me a gift card because she thought I needed a break from my busy schedule. Mrs. Martin is a saint and loves to organize people." Darlin giggled. "Navy wives can be bossy. But I appreciate it."

Amy indicated the dressing room.

Darlin paused inside the door to whisper. "Do I take off all my clothes? Even my underwear?"

"Leave your underwear on if it makes you feel more comfortable," Amy replied. Darlin's eyes were wide with uncertainty as Amy led her into the square relaxation room painted a cream color and furnished with overstuffed sage-colored chairs. Light shone through the curtained windows that faced the ocean, and lavender diffusers added a soothing scent.

Darlin settled into a chair and looked about. A hush filled the room and seemed to make the air thicker. She reclined and sighed. Amy brought her a glass of sparkling water. "The appointment book said you wanted a foot massage?"

"Please."

Amy brought a pitcher of warm water scented with lemon oil. Darlin's eyes closed. "I'm going to pour water over your feet."

"It's lovely to sit and not have anyone asking me for anything." Her eyes flew open. "I don't mean to complain."

Amy poured the water into the basin. "Is the temperature okay?"

"Perfect." Her eyes closed again. Five minutes later Amy brought a warm fluffy towel and gently took Darlin's right foot in her hand to dry.

The woman giggled. "I don't think anyone has washed my feet since my wedding day. My husband is a pastor, and he thought it would be spiritual and romantic for him to wash my feet during the ceremony. Mama did not approve, but it was beautiful and such a loving symbol."

Amy looked up. A soft blush covered the woman's cheeks, but she continued to talk. "How about you? Do you give your husband a massage all the time?"

Amy shook her head. "No husband, not even a boyfriend. Work fills my time now, but maybe someday."

Why did that guy Josh's face pop into her mind? Amy chased the image away and escorted Darlin to the therapy room.

Darlin hesitated in the doorway and glanced at the three candles glowing on the cupboard opposite. Providing ambiance, as well as a warm scent of orange blossoms, the candles supplied most of the light in the dimmed room.

"What happens now?" Darlin whispered.

"Take off the robe and slip under the warmed blanket and

sheet, lying on your stomach. Position your shoulders at the end of the table and place your head in the face cradle." Amy indicated a doughnut-shaped attachment sticking out from the end of the padded massage table in the middle of the room.

"Your forehead goes on the curved edge of the cradle farthest from the table with your nose and mouth in the hole. This will enable you to breathe comfortably while I'm working on your back."

Darlin nodded.

"You'll need to remove the cross from your neck."

Darlin clutched the gold necklace. "But I never take this off. It's a symbol of my faith."

Amy motioned to her necklace. "I feel the same way about mine, but you need to remove it so I can massage your shoulders. I'll step outside while you prepare."

As always, Amy prayed before beginning her job. "Please, Lord, give me discernment and insight into what this sweet woman wants. Help her to relax and get all she needs from our session."

When Darlin answered her knock with a timid okay, Amy reentered the room. "I'm your servant for the next fifty minutes."

Starting on Darlin's left foot and leg, Amy ran her hands down the length of Darlin's leg several times feeling for an evenness in the woman's muscles. She kneaded the ball of the foot, felt several sensitive spots, and rubbed in firm circular motions.

"Marvelous," Darlin murmured.

As she worked, Amy kept her voice at a murmuring level, calming and soothing with the few words she spoke.

"I could get used to this," Darlin murmured.

Amy smiled. Calming the fearful and rubbing away the aches and pains; Amy felt born for the job.

She just had to steel her mind not to fret about how actually to get to work.

* * *

As soon as they squared away the kayak, Josh and Pete crossed Silver Strand Boulevard, showed their IDs to the sentry at the gate, and headed to their team building. There they changed into their uniforms—blue and black urban camouflage—in the locker room before heading to the chow hall on base.

Josh pushed his teal-colored tray behind Pete as they filled their plates with eggs, bacon, toast, oatmeal, coffee, and orange juice. Half their sixteen-man platoon sat at a long table near the door.

"Hail, the Eagle has landed, and he brought Cubby with him," said a muscular man with a red mustache sitting at the end of the table.

"Thanks for letting us sleep in, Chief." Pete set down his tray.

"How long did it take you Boy Scouts to get here?"

Josh checked his watch. "Twenty-seven minutes, Chief Rossi."

"I thought you could do it in twenty minutes."

"Boat's rusty; we've been gone too long."

Chief grunted.

Josh sat beside Flip. A slight-framed man who ate like he never got seconds, Flip never put on an ounce of weight and swam like the dolphin his nickname suggested. SEALs rarely used their real names, preferring the anonymity of an alias.

They called Pete "Eagle," in reference to his teenage rank as an Eagle Scout. Josh was an Eagle Scout, too, but since he was shorter than Pete and preferred not to drink, smoke, or carouse in typical commando fashion, he'd earned the moniker "Cubby" for Cub Scout. They also called him Doc, of course, because he was the trained medic in the platoon.

"You'll have most of the summer to get it shipshape," Chief said. "We'll be training around town this week, gone for a couple weeks, and then in port awhile."

"There's no place like home," Josh said. They'd been away for nearly a month. "Any chance of leave?"

"No. If you want to head north to find mama bear in the big woods, Cubby, you'll have to make it a fast weekend trip."

Josh chewed on a piece of whole-wheat toast and thought about his parents' home outside Boonville in Mendocino County. There he could relax among the redwood trees, hike up the ridge looking toward the coast, and take a walk through the apple orchard with his best friend. With any luck he'd get to hear his father, the senior elder, preach at the small church in town. Tempting. If he flew up late on Friday and came back late on Sunday he could get thirty-six hours away from operational tempo.

"Nothing any time soon, Doc. You'll be training at Balboa through Thursday next week."

Balboa Naval Hospital was the major military teaching hospital on the West Coast. Josh occasionally pulled refresher training at the hospital complex in Balboa Park north of downtown, but hadn't been there in nearly a year. He'd have to borrow Pete's car or take the bus, so he raised his eyebrows at his roommate.

"You can have the keys. Just bring me back a burrito for dinner."

"Tarzan" sat across the table and snickered. "When are you going to be old enough to buy a car, Cubby?"

"As long as Eagle lets me borrow his car, I don't need one. Why spend the money?"

Tarzan leaned forward on the table. He looked like Johnny Weissmuller from the old movies, thus the name. "You don't drink, you don't own a car, you don't smoke, and you don't have a girl. What do you do with all your money? You must be rolling in it."

"I get by."

"Orphans in Mexico," Pete said.

Josh elbowed him.

"You're going to ruin our image if you run around doing a good turn daily," Tarzan said. "We're supposed to be intimidating and brave, not helpful, clean, and reverent."

"Sounds like you know the Boy Scout motto." Josh picked up a piece of bacon with his fingers and took a bite.

"My kid's involved. You gotta learn stuff."

"It's where I got my start. You might be able to show the kids in his troop a thing or two, knots maybe."

"Now there's a thought. I wonder what the den mother would think if I brought our toys over to demonstrate?"

"Rocketry was popular when I was in scouts. We liked to blow things up. Look where I am now."

Tarzan snickered. "Headed to play with the nurses while we learn how to fire specialized mortars. I wonder who's gonna have more fun."

Josh shrugged. Training away from the platoon meant he'd have to catch up, but Pete would help. That's what teammates did for each other.

The rest of the day went in typical fashion: training, a team meeting, razzing the new guys, filing travel claims, and equipment cleaning. At 1630—4:30 p.m. for civilians—they knocked off for the weekend with plenty of time for Josh to walk into town to church. The Friday night meeting for adult singles always included a meal and usually a social event, as well as a Bible study. He hadn't been since April and was looking forward to it.

But it didn't start until six thirty, so Josh changed into civilian clothes and headed to the beach for some time alone.

As Josh cleared the building, he saw the BUD/S class— Basic Underwater Demolition/SEALs course—on the shore. He perched on the sand berm and watched as the trainees hoping to become SEALs tried to keep up with the demanding orders from the instructors. The eight-man teams hauled 170-pound black rubber boats balanced on their heads up and down the beach.

As they drew nearer to Josh, he heard a command and the men dropped their boats, flipped them over, and grabbed the rope on the outside to plunge into the cold Pacific Ocean rolling onto shore. Two boat crews floundered as they hit the first wave, and the men flew into the air before falling into the surf. Six other boats made it past the white water and headed to sea. Josh knew the buoy they paddled toward and wished them well.

He'd taken his turn five years before, entering into the twenty-eight-week BUD/S training camp with the ignorant gusto of a strong young man. Pushed to his physical and mental limits, he had limped through without any serious injury except to his soul. The orders were raw, the language ugly, the hours long, the physical tasks nearly unendurable.

He'd spent most of his time wet, sandy, hungry, cold, and always tired. Never enough time to sleep and never enough energy to do all required, it took fortitude and true grit to get through the training. He had no idea how many sit-ups and push-ups he'd done, but he knew he was stronger and more determined afterward.

No time off and the ocean never stopped moving, cold and unfriendly. Pushed to the limit, always urged to win, BUD/S sapped everything a man had and more. Without his mother's prayers, he never would have made it.

Josh was grateful he'd never have to experience anything like the SEAL training pipeline again.

Except, of course, it prepared him for the job he performed in often worse and more dangerous conditions. SEALs liked to say the only easy day was yesterday.

An easy day yesterday, sure, but not earlier in the week. Getting trapped in a narrow underwater tunnel on Monday was one of the most unnerving situations he'd ever encountered. A civilian diver had panicked and nearly drowned before their eyes. The whole squad, and Flip especially, had a hard time with the incident, even after yesterday's debrief. As the platoon medic, Josh would need to keep an eye on Flip as well as the other three men with him that day.

Josh sat on the sand and reached into the pocket of his backpack for a small camouflage-covered New Testament, a gift from his mother. He only carried it while home on Coronado; having a Bible with him on the job was unthinkable. If he were captured with it in some of the places Josh had infiltrated, he would be killed on the spot.

If the bad guys could capture him. No SEAL had ever been captured or left behind. They fought to the death. Anything else was unacceptable.

Josh passed a weary hand across his forehead. The job was so soul sapping. He wasn't sure if his heart was back in the right place with God or not, though he'd certainly been trying. Maybe tonight would show him the truth. The book of James was always good for the soul.

Chapter 7

Lindsey arrived for her spa appointment early and settled into the relaxation room with a catlike purr. Amy had given her massages in the past, so when the time came to enter the therapy room, she thought she knew what to expect. Lindsey, however, had been perusing the spa menu and wanted to experience several new techniques.

Jackie, who knew Lindsey was also a massage therapist, joined them to demonstrate, and the three women were laughing before too long.

"Shh," Jackie admonished them. "This is a relaxing place, laughter is too loud."

"My fault," Lindsey said. "I'm too used to athletes and their simple needs. All these aromatic choices are making me feel giddy."

Amy selected slow Bach music to calm her "client" and leaned hard on the spots where Lindsey knotted up. By the time she finished, a limp Lindsey could barely crawl to the dressing room. As soon as Lindsey changed into her swimsuit, Amy led her to the whirlpool.

"How long do I have?" Lindsey asked as she climbed into the water.

"I get off at six." Amy snagged a stray white towel and dumped it in the hamper.

"I'm treating for dinner." Lindsey yawned. "Assuming I ever move again."

"When you're done in here, try the pool. The view over the ocean is spectacular."

Amy's final hour of the workday was at poolside, serving drinks and catering to the client's needs. She gratefully pushed open the glass doors into the private pool area. With the sun shining down and the glass walls protecting the area from chilling ocean breezes, serenity reigned. White chaise lounges, a fire pit, and the blue infinity pool made for a relaxing spot. Sweet William flowers surrounded daisies in a large planter, and their scent lingered in the air.

She saw Lindsey floating in the pool and chatting with Darlin, her client from earlier in the day.

Amy checked her watch. "You're still here, Darlin?"

"I'm stringing this along to the very hour I have to leave. My husband is in charge of everything tonight and will pick me up at six. Dinner is taken care of; kids are off for the night. Total luxury. I feel spoiled."

"Can you suggest a place for dinner? Lindsey's treating me." Amy straightened the pillow on the chaise beside Darlin and picked up several empty glasses.

Darlin sat up straight herself. "You girls should come with us to our weekly potluck for folks your age. We get mostly military and some summer help, but it's your demographic, and the guys are cute." She lowered her voice. "They outnumber the women and are very good looking."

Lindsey waved her glass of iced tea. "I'm in. How about it, Amy? You can be my cheap date."

"Where are we going?"

"Potluck dinner tonight at our church with an introduction

to the book of James," Darlin said. "We meet together for the potluck; figure out small group Bible study meeting times for the summer, and then do something fun. Dinner will be free and don't bring anything, we always have enough."

Amy considered Darlin's expectant face. "What sort of church? I'm a Lutheran."

"We're a nondenominational group that meets downtown. Everyone's welcome to join us."

As she arranged the empty glasses on a tray, Amy thought about the invitation. She was tired from work, but not exhausted. It might be fun to meet new people and see a little of the legendary Coronado nightlife. Lindsey was driving, and she didn't have to worry about crossing the bridge alone.

"Why not?"

She met the two women outside the front entrance to the Hotel Del after work. Amy wore a pale green knit dress and tan flip-flops with miniature palm trees sprinkled across the straps. She carried a lightweight sweater over her arm for the cooling evening.

Lindsey and Darlin had changed into street clothes of course, with Lindsey in a teal summer dress and black flip-flops. With her red hair brushed back into a black velvet band, her face shone fresh and healthy.

"You both look delightful," Darlin said. "I told Lindsey you two should ride with me since parking is difficult downtown. We'll bring you back afterward. It shouldn't go later than nine." She winked at them. "After the marvelous day I've had, I'll be tugging Wayne home early, but everyone can stay later if they want. Besides, it's Friday night."

"We have to work in the morning. Nine will be fine for me," Amy said.

"How are you getting to work tomorrow?" Lindsey asked.

"Traffic should be light on Saturday. I'll drive around through Imperial Beach." She made a face.

Darlin watched her. "What's wrong with the bridge?"

Amy shuddered.

Lindsey rubbed Amy's arm in sympathy. "She can't drive the bridge. It's too scary. She nearly killed herself the one time she tried."

"Where do you girls live?"

"Up near San Diego State. About twenty miles, but with the downtown traffic it can be a long trip. It took me nearly an hour to get here for my interview," Amy said.

"It'll be even longer if you have to drive south to Imperial Beach and go up around the bay. How long is that trip?"

"More than thirty miles." She tried to smile. "It's nice to know I can go to an evening Bible study at your church Friday nights if I want to stay late and avoid traffic."

"You can come to church tomorrow night, too. With all the summer help working on Sundays, we have a Saturday night service at six thirty." Darlin pointed at a hotel manager walking by. "He just started coming."

Lindsey watched after him. "You're tempting me to look for a job on Coronado."

Amy felt a surge of hope. "Would you?"

She shook her head. "My life is on the other side of San Diego."

Amy nodded. Even though she loved her new job and was optimistic about the money she'd earn, a large part of her heart wished she, too, had a well-paying job near home and San Diego State.

Josh pulled the windbreaker out of his backpack, replaced the tiny New Testament, and prepared to walk to town. It wasn't far, and he had plenty of time. Watching the men training on the beach, looking through his New Testament, and praying about his life for the first concentrated time in weeks left him feeling refreshed and clean. The outdoors always helped him gain perspective, and he was grateful.

Beaches in California were open to anyone who wanted

to walk on them, and Josh preferred the water anyway, so he trudged through the sand past the utilitarian buildings of the west side of the navy base. Tall apartment houses faced the beach a little farther north, and then he reached the splendor of the Hotel Del Coronado's beachfront. The sturdy white hotel with a red roof had graced the shores for more than 120 years and looked magnificent from the water.

Actually, the sprawling Victorian hotel looked magnificent from any direction, and it had given Josh inspiration those nights he battled the cold waves during his BUD/S training. He remembered the shock on tourists' faces when the trainees in his class had tried to land their rubber rafts on a line of rocks at the south end of the beach.

He and his six-man boat crew had ridden a high wave up and nearly foundered. Someone lassoed a boulder with a line and tied them off, enabling his boat crew to escape the pounding sea. The drill instructor standing on the topmost rock yelled at them, but finally agreed they had performed properly. They'd pulled their rubber boat off the rocks and collapsed on the sand, the tourists staggering back in horror. So tired he could barely move, in the darkness of the beach Josh had cricked his neck to stare at the bright gaudy lights of the hotel.

BUD/S had been so tough he sometimes barely felt human, but that night staring at the hotel, he'd remembered the pleasures of comfort, warmth, and a good meal, and he swore he'd survive. He'd have to get a room there one night, maybe for his parents. They had a military rate.

Josh cut across the sand to the north side of the green lawn in front of the broad original hotel and followed a sidewalk through the complex. He paused when he saw the double glass doors leading into the spa, the place where Amy worked. He hoped her day had gone well.

When he reached Orange Avenue, Coronado's main drag, he turned left. Three blocks up, he stopped at Bottega Italiana to pick up gelato for dessert. He should get to the wood-sided church just in time for dinner.

Pastor Wayne waited by the church door. "Glad to see you. No Pete?"

"He went to look up a woman he met before we deployed. She lives in Imperial Beach and gets off at six. He'll be in church tomorrow night."

"No pressure. It'll be good to see him again. We've got a pretty full house tonight. Darlin did your spy work for you, by the way. You owe her. She's better than you are."

"No offense, pastor, but that's hard to believe."

"Amy lives near San Diego State. Her mother lives in San Pedro, up in LA, but she has no other relatives. She's majoring in kinesiology and wants to be a physical therapist. Her roommate's name is Lindsey and she's a lot of fun. Oh, and she's Lutheran. Did you need to know anything else?"

Josh grinned. "Does she like baseball?"

"No time to find out. It's a short drive from the Del. She's inside. Ask her yourself."

"I'll play the field first. What's the roommate like?"

"Pretty. She's a massage therapist, too."

"That sounds promising."

"Time to eat." Pastor Wayne greeted several others, and Josh entered the church narthex. A door to the left led to a fellowship hall from which he could smell tomato sauce, spicy salsa, and coffee.

The room held two dozen people, mostly standing near the counter covered with food. Josh sidled to the kitchen and put the gelato containers in the freezer. Carlos, wearing his firefighter's uniform, chatted with three pretty women in a corner. Judging by their hair, Josh figured they must be sailors from one of the North Island ships.

Darlin fluttered among the crowd, stopping to greet newcomers and hug others. When she reached Josh, dimples deepened in her cheeks, and she held out her arms. She smelled like she'd spent the day in a perfume shop, all floral and sweet, but he took the hug. He forgot how soft a woman could be.

"Your friend is here," Darlin whispered. "I like her very much."

Josh glanced across the room and saw Amy. A loop of her sun-streaked hair fell across her cheek as she talked with two local guys. Her smile lit up her face, and her hands moved as she talked. An amused redhead leaned against the wall watching Amy. Josh crossed his arms and wondered at the best approach to cut out the two guys and gain the women's attention for himself.

The surprise element always worked on the job. Hit 'em hard and fast and then get out of there.

The redhead saw him and stood taller. Josh shook hands with a guy who'd been in Bible study with him in the fall. They exchanged the usual nonanswers about work, and then Josh drifted through the room greeting folks until he stood behind Amy.

"Why don't you move to the island for the summer?" one of the guys asked. "Find a place to live and get to know us? Coronado's a great place to live."

"Good idea, Amy," the redhead said. "I've got a friend from Fresno coming down next week for summer school. She could take your half of the rent for the summer, and you could live here. It would solve both your problems: the bridge and the guy."

Amy wrinkled her nose. "Ethan is not a problem, he's just a nuisance. Besides, I couldn't afford a place here."

"We've got some elderly widows at church," one of the locals volunteered. "One of them might have a spot."

"Is Ethan your boyfriend?" the other guy asked. Josh stepped closer.

"He's a guy from school who keeps asking me out." Amy's

lips twitched. "Maybe if I went out with him, he'd get it out of his system and leave me alone."

"I don't think so," the first guy said, echoing Josh's thoughts.

"Listen up," Pastor Wayne called. "We're going to pray and then eat. You'll notice each of the tables is marked with a day of the week. We'll divide you up into small group Bible studies right now, so choose your preferred night and sit down. For you military types with rotating watches, make your best guess. Dinner will be your introduction."

"So, what night will you be taking, Amy?" Josh stepped in front of her as she reached the potluck line.

"You!"

Josh held out his hand to the redhead. "I'm Josh Murphy, Amy's rescuer. Who are you?"

"Lindsey Duncan, lovely to meet you."

Amy's jaw worked up and down like she couldn't decide what to say.

"Did you get home okay on the bus last night? We were concerned about you." Josh reached for cutlery.

"Do you make it a habit of scaring women just for fun?" Amy snatched a paper plate from the stack and held it in front of her like a shield.

"You got across the bridge, didn't you?"

"That doesn't matter."

He put up his hand and stopped her. "You got across the bridge, right?"

"I was so mad at you chasing me I didn't dare get off the bus."

"Chasing you? I was praying for you. It looks like it worked."

"Okay, thanks for the prayers, but you don't get it. The bridge makes me sweat. My skin crawls, I can hardly breathe, and you treat it like a joke." Her voice could be heard over the clash of the cutlery, and one of the local guys grabbed his arm.

"I wouldn't do that if I were you," Josh warned.

"Knock it off. You're upsetting her," the guy said.

"I don't want to make a scene in a church," Amy said. "But I'll call the police if you don't stop making me feel bad. In fact, I'll do it right now." She waved her hands at someone behind Josh. "Officer, can you help me get rid of this guy?"

Josh looked over his shoulder. Carlos frowned as he walked in their direction.

Chapter 8

"That was fun," Lindsey said in a false cheery voice as she turned off Orange Avenue onto Fourth Street, which led to the Coronado Bridge.

"I don't want to talk about it." Amy huddled as far into the bucket seat as she could get, her arm crossed tight across her chest. Her heart hammered as they neared the five-lane-wide canopy—all that remained of the abandoned toll booths—before heading up the bridge. "He was wearing a uniform. How was I supposed to know he was a firefighter and not a police officer?"

"Police officers usually wear boots and have radios. It usually says police on their shirts. I wouldn't worry about it. They all laughed," Lindsey said.

"I'll never be able to show my face at the church again." Even to Amy's ears her voice sounded thin and wistful.

"Don't be silly. They're friendly, and Josh, oh my, Amy, did you look at him?"

"He's the one who causes all the trouble. Every difficult moment I've had on this island was because of him."

Lindsey gunned the engine and sped up the bridge. Amy's stomach dropped and her palms went clammy.

"Don't look. You'll be okay." Lindsey glanced at her.

"Keep your eyes on the road." Amy couldn't tell if she had shrieked or if it just felt like it. Her head pounded and tremors coursed through her body. She closed her eyes.

"Really, Amy, maybe you should see a shrink. You're a mess."

Amy took big breaths, long and slow. She pressed her hands over her face. "Are we there yet?"

"Let's talk about something else. Tell me why you don't like the guy."

"I don't need any guys in my life right now. They cause trouble. I certainly don't have time for a guy who makes me feel miserable at every opportunity."

"I thought it made perfect sense to distract you," Lindsey said. "If you identify your fears and confront them, they won't bother you."

"Really?" Amy peered between her fingers. "What do you think about spiders?"

"Spiders are different. They can kill you. They creep around and spin sticky webs. No thanks. Spiders are scary."

"So are strange guys." Amy squeezed her eyes shut again.

"Are you afraid of Josh?" Lindsey flicked on her blinker and changed lanes.

"Annoyed. I hardly know him after three stupid conversations."

"He looks harmless to me, and he apologized. You met him at church—how bad can he be?"

Amy sighed. "Are we there yet?"

"Coming down the other side. Count to thirty and you'll be fine. Count with me, Ames. One, two..."

At thirty, Amy opened her eyes. The National Avenue off-ramp sloped to the right. She was back on land. They should be home within twenty minutes, and she could take a shower before falling blissfully into sleep. She could hardly wait.

"What time will you leave tomorrow?" Lindsey asked.

"Logically it should only take an hour to drive around, but to make sure I'm going to give it ninety minutes. I'll leave around seven fifteen."

"That will be a long day," Lindsey said. "Especially if you stay for church."

"I'm never going back to that church."

"Suit yourself, but I think I'll go back. Josh is really good looking. Maybe it's those Irish genes—black hair, clear blue eyes, and lopsided grin, oh my."

"You can have him," Amy said. "He's nothing but trouble, and he's perfectly capable of killing you, literally, with one hand. He told me so. Or maybe Pete did."

"Pete? I don't think I met him."

"Darlin said he'd be at church tomorrow night."

The lights of downtown San Diego flashed by in a friendly fashion, much more comforting than the twinkling lights of the Coronado Bridge. Amy relaxed. Other than the absurd scene with Josh, the evening had been fun. The potluck food was delicious, the people friendly, the Bible study interesting, and it all felt so welcoming. If only Josh hadn't shown up.

"Did Darlin tip you this afternoon?" Lindsey asked.

Amy perked up. "Twenty dollars."

"She should have tipped you more. She used a gift card for her massage."

Amy shook her head. "You didn't tip me anything."

"I took you out to dinner."

"You took me to a potluck where you didn't have to bring anything and where a navy guy made fun of me."

Lindsey shrugged. "You've got an opportunity because we went to the potluck. You need to go to church there tomorrow night and get friendly with Darlin. I bet she knows if someone has a place to stay. If you could swing a summer rental, Amy, your life would be easier."

"Are you trying to get rid of me?"

"No," Lindsey said. "I only want the best for you. If you won't get help for your bridge phobia, not crossing it makes sense."

Amy shook her head. "Everything is expensive on Coronado. I doubt I could find anything as cheap as our apartment."

She watched the freeway signs flash by as they journeyed home: 75 to US 5 to US 15 to US 8. She'd reverse them tomorrow morning. It took many roads, intersections, and miles to get to her job at the fabulous Del. Both the ferry and the bus commutes took ninety minutes each way. Maybe a job at the Del was reaching too high? Maybe she should give up and find work closer to home and not have to commute?

But Amy remembered the healthy tips on top of her salary. The opportunities at the Del were huge. "I'm not going to let my fear beat me," she whispered. She pulled out her cell phone and looked at the time. Maybe Mama could advise her.

SEALs did most of their work at night, across time lines, and with little warning. Josh learned early on to fall asleep at will and whenever he had the opportunity. Problem was, he might be able to fall asleep, but he always woke with the dawn, even when he didn't want to.

The apartment he shared with Pete above the Calloways' garage had windows facing both east and west. Josh had taken the tiny west-facing bedroom and slept with the windows open to catch the ocean breeze coming from a mere eight blocks away. He awoke Saturday morning to a world smothered in gray fog, lying low and damp on the ground. He could barely make out the wide fronds of the palm tree beside the street not thirty feet away. A thick marine soup, perfect for clandestine operations, but nothing was on the agenda.

At least he didn't think so.

Josh stretched into sweats, tied on his shoes, and crept out of the apartment. He loved to run in a murky mist.

The moist air swirled around him as he ran in the street against nonexistent traffic. He smelled the brine of the sea and blinked back droplets of fog. Houses loomed like dark ghosts as Josh picked up the pace under the smoldering streetlights. Coronado Island lay quiet and still. His sensitive ears could pick up few sounds save the distant rumble of waves on the beach.

"Holy, holy, holy," he hummed to himself. "Early in the morning my song shall rise to thee." The long hours in unpleasant places waiting for the enemy had given him plenty to think and pray about over the years. Sunrises over mountains, peeking rays appearing in a burst on desert plains; he'd waited and watched and while not exactly able to let his mind drift, Josh had developed the habit of praying with half of his brain and staying alert with the other. It worked well in dangerous situations like ambushing bad guys...or avoiding vicious dogs.

A black dog rushed at him, barking loud enough to wake the neighbors. Josh stopped and crouched to eye level. "Come here, boy."

The dog wasn't so sure anymore and wavered, his bark slowing, muffling, and finally whimpering to a tail wag. Josh scratched his ears. "You go home now. It's not safe for dogs to be out this early."

"Rascal?" a voice shouted in the dark.

Josh tugged on the dog's collar and inserted him into the right yard. "Just doing today's good turn."

And then he sobered, remembering yesterday's conversation. It hadn't gone well.

He jogged back to rhythm. Tarzan hadn't wanted to talk about Boy Scouts; he preferred to pick on Josh. He'd been complaining a lot recently, insisting Josh wasn't a good teammate if he didn't join them at the bar.

Josh blew out his cheeks. Could he help it if he preferred the apple cider he'd grown up drinking rather than beer? He didn't like the taste, and he didn't like the buzz. What he liked the least was the lack of control. No telling what he'd say if he had a couple of beers. Josh steered clear for a reason.

But not a good enough one for Tarzan and a couple of the other guys, and they didn't like Josh's jokes on the subject either. In trying to stay true to who he was, he'd managed to insult half the team. "What should I do, Lord?"

Even as he jogged down the street, he knew the answer. It was probably time to make his quarterly visit to the favorite hangout, McP's. He'd stop in on his way to church tonight. Maybe someone would join him at church? Flip could benefit from attending with Josh; he'd been moody ever since they got back from the Gulf.

Josh shook his head. More likely he'd get punched in the mouth from one of his teammates if he even suggested church. He'd probably deserve it, too. Josh couldn't seem to keep his mouth shut in social settings, as witnessed by every stupid thing he'd said to Amy.

His frustration made him pick up the pace, and soon he had reached Orange Avenue. He ran until he reached the Hotel Del, a shining Victorian wedding cake disappearing in the mist.

Josh turned the corner and ran past the hotel toward the water. Maybe he'd see how the BUD/S class was doing south of the hotel.

Visibility was near zero when he got to the beach and Josh slowed to a walk. He knew this stretch of sand like the back of his hand; all SEALs did. Past the tall apartment buildings shrouded dark on a Saturday morning, past the buildings of NAB, he went. When he got to the SEAL compound with its razor-wire fence, he pulled the military ID from his brown shirt pocket and handed it to the guard.

A flashlight examined the laminated card and then flashed at Josh's face. "What are you up to, Murphy?"

"Morning jog."

"Have a good one." The guard returned his ID.

Josh continued down the beach, listening for the trainees. He heard their shout: "Hooyah, Mr. Spangler."

With arms linked, sixty men sat in the water, the waves rolling as high as their chins, sweeping past them to the beach, and then rolling out again. Ten SEAL instructors wearing black shorts and brown shirts patrolled the beach shouting discouraging comments at the men. Josh knew how cold they felt, a bone-chilling stutter that stayed for hours. One instructor held a stopwatch. Hypothermia kicked in after twenty minutes. They usually pulled the trainees out around nineteen.

"Get sandy," the instructor yelled. The trainees mustered out of the water and rolled, covering their soaking wet white shirts and camouflage pants with gritty sand. When a whistle blew, they picked up their rubber boats and headed farther inland to the obstacle course. Josh followed at a distance; the fog gave him cover.

Watching the men do push-ups on command and then start on the obstacle course, Josh estimated they had three or four weeks until Hell Week, a five-day period of miserable orders during which no one got any sleep. Hell Week usually broke those who weren't absolutely determined to be a SEAL. It was brutal, men sometimes died, and no one ever forgot it. Josh merged into the shadows. He'd need to find out who the angels were going to be during this class's Hell Week.

When he exited the compound and reached Silver Strand Boulevard, Josh crossed with the traffic light. He joined the broad bike path, built on the right of way for the 1888 railroad, and ran to town. He had his hopes set on a smoothie from Café 1134, along with a full breakfast.

He pushed through the front door, damp but happy. The scent of coffee pervaded the air, along with scrambled eggs, toast, and home fries. He took a seat at the counter and ordered breakfast.

"I should buy you a drink." Carlos set his half-eaten plate on the counter and hooked the chair with his foot to sit down.

"What kind of drinks do you buy on a Saturday morning?"

"It's a French restaurant. You want a latte?"

Josh shook his head. "Sailors drink real coffee."

"Cappuccino, espresso? Name your poison."

"I'll take a fresh-squeezed orange juice. Why do you owe me a drink?"

Two thumbs up. "Amy and Lindsey were mighty fine. I'm glad you pushed her into my arms."

"You firefighters have a savior complex. It was only fitting."

Carlos leaned his elbows on the table. "Maybe we could work out a code. I'll give you a secret sign, and you say something stupid, forcing the pretty girls to turn to me for help."

"Whatever works. I'm at your service." Josh sighed. "I didn't mean to upset her, but she's a spitfire when she's angry. I like it." He thanked the waitress for the juice.

"I hope you didn't scare her away, but her girlfriend will probably bring her back. She liked what she saw in our church."

"Which small group did you join?"

"Friday night. How about you?"

Josh lifted his glass. "Wouldn't miss it. Think they'll be at church tonight?"

"Only if you didn't scare them away."

Chapter 9

Was driving in the fog any better than taking the bridge? Amy peered out the windshield of her car. She couldn't see anything more than ten feet ahead of her hood as the traffic crawled down Silver Strand Boulevard. She might as well be on the bridge, since she couldn't see anything.

No, she would have known. Thinking about all the air underneath the bridge roadway made her shiver even as she drove on the highway at sea level. Driving around was the better choice, this time.

Amy got to work early. The thick mist was too damp for a comfortable walk on the beach, so she settled herself in the empty relaxation room. She had her little Gideon's Bible, and she'd prepare her heart for the day. Amy could perform her job better if she started her day calm. With the weather so socked in, the schedule probably would be full.

"You did a good job yesterday. Darlin suggested you to a friend." Kathy put her thumbs up. "It's one of our special ladies. Do you know how to do compassionate touch?"

"The gentle massage for elderly people? Yes. How old is the client?"

"Mrs. Martin is older than the hills. Her family's been on Coronado since the beginning, and she lives in a huge house with a view of San Diego. She's a widow. Her husband was an admiral, and she won't let you forget it."

"Do you know her?" Amy asked.

"She comes in often for a massage. Her daughter, Susan, lives up by UCSD where she's a professor. She comes down on the weekends to take over for the caregiver," Kathy said. "I think she brings Mrs. Martin in so she can run errands."

"Maybe the daughter needs a massage?"

"Probably, but the two hours Mrs. Martin stays with us gives Susan time to herself. We do a gentle massage, coddle her, and serve tea. She's a character."

Amy liked Mrs. Martin the moment she swept in with her middle-aged daughter, who looked as prim and competent as every math teacher Amy had known. Susan helped her mother into a white robe, dutifully kissed her on the cheek, and said good-bye. "I'll return for lunch at one. We have a reservation at Sheerwater Restaurant."

"Did you ask for a view?" Mrs. Martin asked.

"Don't I always?" Susan gave Amy a tight-lipped smile and fled.

The diminutive Adelaide Josephine Crocker Martin had eloped at the age of eighteen with a dashing navy flyer stationed at North Island the third year of World War II. A hero during the war, Hiram—"High"—Martin had continued up the chain of command, leading men and flying navy planes for twenty-five years more. They had lived all over the world and hobnobbed with celebrities and minor royalty. Amy heard the whole story within minutes of meeting the eighty-eight-year-old woman with still-beautiful skin.

"My mother knew Wallis Simpson, you know." Mrs. Martin handed a carved teak cane to Amy as she arranged herself in the overstuffed pale green love seat in the relaxation room. "She didn't approve of the woman."

"I'm sorry; I don't know who she is." Amy set the cane aside.

Mrs. Martin drew herself up as regally as a queen. "Are you educated?"

"I just finished my junior year at San Diego State. I'm majoring in kinesiology."

"Ah, physical movement. Perhaps you are unacquainted with the history of the British monarchy?"

"You mean like Prince William and Queen Elizabeth? Not much beyond them. Who is Wallis Simpson?"

"She married Prince Edward, the current queen's late uncle, in the 1930s. He gave up the throne to marry Wallis, who was a divorcée, and they lived the rest of their lives in the south of France. Mother said—well, never mind. There's no point in gossiping about old scandal. I will have a cup of Earl Grey tea, please, no sugar."

Amy spent the next two hours with the chatty, intelligent woman. Once she finished her tea, they moved to a therapy room. "Hands, arms, feet, and lower legs today, and I want that orange blossom scent," Mrs. Martin said.

Amy looked through the massage oils. "Do you ever have facials, Mrs. Martin?" She turned to see the woman staring at her.

"Do I look like I need a facial?"

Amy thought fast. "I asked because your complexion is gorgeous for a woman…"

"As old as I am?"

Amy gave up. "Sure. What do you use to look so beautiful?"

Mrs. Martin put her head back and laughed. "Well done. I have taken care of myself ever since I was a girl with regular facials, massages, and elegant treatments all over the world. My mother told me if I wanted to keep a man as distinguished as High, I needed to be as beautiful as he liked. So I was. I'm not sure why Susan never learned to do the same."

Amy gazed at the sprightly woman. Her blue eyes gleamed against her pale complexion and her white hair glowed with health and vigor. Even in the spa, Mrs. Martin wore bright red lipstick, and her nails were beautifully manicured. "I hope I'm as healthy and lovely as you are when I'm half your age," Amy said.

"You will if you have a life as interesting as mine, and if you take care of yourself."

Amy picked up the woman's soft hand. "I'll try."

Compassionate touch therapy involves moving slowly and gently over thin skin. Amy's mother had many elderly clients, and Amy had observed the care and time it took to make a person feel like the therapist had connected with them, not only physically, but emotionally. It's often the only time many elderly people got any physical contact.

She began by slowly moving her thumb in a circling motion on Mrs. Martin's right palm. Before long, the woman sighed and leaned back. Amy knew she had found the right stroke.

"A massage and prayer are the best things in life," Mrs. Martin murmured.

The time gently massaging, chatting, and seeing to Mrs. Martin's comfort was Amy's most satisfying appointment in months.

Josh sat on the wall outside of the spa waiting for six o'clock to arrive and Amy to leave the building. He wasn't sure she would speak to him, but he needed to apologize.

He saw her exit the double glass doors with a cute girl. Did she only have cute girlfriends? He thought about forgetting it, but the set of Amy's mouth convinced him he needed to speak.

"Listen, Amy."

"I don't want to talk to you." She turned her head away.

"I can understand why. I came to tell you I'm sorry. I didn't mean to hurt your feelings."

The other girl looked between them. "Is this a private conversation?"

"Please stay, Jackie. I don't want to be alone with him." Amy narrowed her eyes. "He's a walking time bomb." She pressed her lips into a straight line.

The friend, Jackie, raised her eyebrows. "What did you do?"

"Nothing. She's perfectly safe with me, but feel free to stay. I wasn't careful with my words, Amy, and I can understand why you may not want to talk to me. I wanted to tell you I'm sorry. What I said was out of line and not empathetic. Will you forgive me?"

She dropped her chin and stared at him. "Did you say empathetic? Do you even know what it means?"

"Technically." He dropped his hands. "To put yourself into someone else's shoes and understand how she is feeling. I didn't even try to be sympathetic yesterday. I tried to rationally talk you out of your fear. I was wrong. People are entitled to their feelings. I'm sorry."

"Sounds good to me," Jackie said.

Josh put his hands together. "I need to clear the decks. Will you forgive me? I'll leave you alone and not bother you anymore if I can have your forgiveness."

Amy looked past him toward the ocean, where large waves crashed on the shore as the sun sank toward the horizon. He watched her face crinkle and smooth. Silence lengthened and he stood perfectly still. He knew how to wait.

"Aren't you going to say anything?" Jackie prodded Amy's shoulder with an open hand. "He sounds sorry to me."

Amy shifted her backpack from one hand to the next. Josh could smell the clean floral scent from the spa, or was it from her hair? Her fresh appearance belied a long workday but he knew she must be tired.

"I keep coming back to empathetic." She glared at him. "Do you want to be empathetic?"

Josh's senses went on danger alert. What was she asking?

"Do you want to know what it feels like to be me? How terrified I am when I see the bridge? Don't you think it might help if you tried to understand why someone could be afraid?"

It was Josh's turn to look away. He wouldn't mind knowing more about Amy, but becoming sympathetic to other people's feelings might weaken him. He couldn't give a lot of thought to a bad guy as a person, even though Josh knew all men were created in God's image for His purposes.

"Maybe."

"You're hopeless," she spit. "Absolutely hopeless. You don't care anything about me, why bother to ask for forgiveness? No. I won't forgive you."

"Amy!" Jackie gasped.

Josh froze inside, a bone-chilling cold worse than anything he had felt sitting in freezing water up to his neck in BUD/S training. He wanted to shake her but instead, sadness washed over him. His shoulders slumped. This situation was wrong, and his words had caused it.

She continued. "You're not sorry. You're just trying to clear your soul, but if your heart isn't in the right place, it won't work. Ask me when you're willing to change your attitude."

"I am sorry. I know I hurt you. What can I do to show you I'll try not to say anything bad about your fears again?"

"Why don't you come down to the beach with us?" Jackie said. "You two can discuss your problem in a more relaxed setting."

"Jackie!" Amy cried.

"The guy said he was sorry. I don't know what your issue is, but you're obviously not in agreement. You should talk it out. Why don't you come with us to the bonfire? It's a party for the college-age summer help: drinks, hot dogs, probably s'mores. We'll tell them you're Amy's date."

"No we won't," Amy snapped.

"Okay." Jackie smiled at Josh. "He can be my date. Let's go."

Amy grabbed Josh's arm, and he jerked at the touch. "He'll be with me. There's no telling who he'll insult if I'm not there to intervene."

"You're not going to church?" Josh asked.

She dropped her hand. "Fine. Go to church. Be holy. I told my coworkers I'd join them tonight." Amy looked uncertain and spoke more gently. "I'll probably go to your church next week. Will you come with us, or are you going to let the sun go down on my anger?"

"I'll come."

Her strong hand drew him like a hot magnet as she tugged him toward the beach. Josh followed without a word, hopeful yet resigned. He doubted he'd enjoy a party on the beach with college students, particularly when he could finally go to church, but maybe he could gain insight into the beautiful, infuriating woman by his side.

Beautiful? Cute, sure, but where did beautiful come from? Josh darted a glance in her direction.

Her determined face caught his movement. "Don't look at me. You're not forgiven yet."

Josh bit back a smile. Maybe not yet, but it would come. She'd forgive him someday. And he, at least, could go to church tomorrow knowing he had tried.

Chapter 10

Amy marched up to Marty, the guy who had invited her, and introduced Josh. She couldn't help comparing them as Josh put out his hand and Marty reluctantly shook it. The thin bellhop, whom she knew went to UC San Diego, looked diminished beside Josh with his muscular body, tanned skin, and flashing blue eyes.

"You a friend of Amy's?" Marty asked.

"A sort of brother." Josh nodded toward the fire. "You guys do this often?"

"What do you mean?"

"I was a Boy Scout. Let's see if I can help you with this fire." Josh picked up a long piece of wood and adjusted the burning logs by propping several on end to create a teepee shape. Flames leaped as he worked, and the roar of the fire could almost be heard over the crashing waves.

Once he got it going well, Josh stepped away from the fire and looked around.

Marty grunted. "Who knew?" He reached into a cooler, pulled out a can, and gave it to Amy. "Have a drink. Is your brother from around here? You don't look like him."

"I watch after her like a brother. No relation. You got a bottle of water in your cooler?" Josh asked. "I don't like the hard stuff."

Amy returned the can to Marty. "I don't either. Can I have a Diet Coke?"

Marty pointed to the other side of the fire. "Suit yourself. It's in the blue cooler by the food."

She walked with Josh over to the food. "Were you really a Boy Scout?"

"Eagle, Troop 175, Ukiah, California, a long time ago."

"Did anything you learned in Scouts transfer to your job other than fire building? Things like being kind to ladies?"

He laughed. "Of course. Hey, Jackie, got anything to eat?"

Jackie helped a plump blond from housekeeping set food out on a table brought from the hotel. "You'll need to cook your own hot dog, but you know your way around a fire. I doubt you'll have any trouble."

He didn't. As Amy mingled with her coworkers, all college kids working at the Del for the summer, she couldn't help contrasting Josh's calm assurance—and skill— with the others. He teased the girls, joked with the guys, and blended in like a chameleon. The more she watched him, the less sure she was about her anger.

The night turned cool the way it always did at the beach in California, and Amy put on the blue fleece from her backpack. Others pulled on outer garments but not Josh. He stood around the fire, his finely sculpted muscles obvious in his button-down white shirt. She shouldn't have made him miss church, she realized. Still, he looked perfectly at home, perfectly friendly, perfectly...on the alert?

Where did the word *alert* come from? Amy surveyed the dozen folks sitting around the fire. They looked harmless.

Marty pulled out a guitar and plucked quietly on the strings. "Navy's out tonight."

"Always spoiling the beaches," said another bellhop they

called Steve. He lit a cigarette. "Night and day they're out there showing off to the tourists."

Amy met Josh's eyes. He shook his head at her but otherwise was motionless. One word described him: alert.

"Will you make a marshmallow for me, Josh?" asked the blond from housekeeping. He took the roasting fork and slipped on two marshmallows, gazing into the fire as if he had nothing better to do.

Sparks flew up from the smoky bonfire. Overhead the first stars of the evening prickled the sky, and the moon rose full and golden in the east.

"I'm a pacifist myself," Steve said. "We should spend military money on schools and poor people. But don't say that too loudly around here. Coronado is a military town, and they love the navy."

Marty took the sweet-smelling cigarette from him and dragged on it. "SEALs are the worst. All body, no brain; they're nothing but Rambos in camouflage. They'd never cut it in the intelligence department."

A muscled tightened in Josh's cheek. He handed the perfectly roasted marshmallows back to the waiting blond and put out his hand in Amy's direction. "Time to go."

She faced her colleagues. "Thanks for the fun evening. I'll see you tomorrow at work. Are you coming, Jackie?"

"I'll help clean up. Don't forget your first appointment isn't until noon. You get to sleep in!"

In a dream, perhaps spun of beach sand or marshmallow sugar, Amy slipped on her backpack and took Josh's hand. Heat and a buzz spilled between their fingers and his grip tightened.

"You don't have to work until noon?" he asked.

"Right, that's why I didn't go to church tonight. I'm sorry I made you miss the service."

"I can go tomorrow. Let's walk by the water. I want to talk to you."

His hand felt so strong and firm, confident, as she followed him toward the water. Amy struggled to catch her breath. Was she feeling the actual blood running like fire from his touch? "Okay."

"There's an example of demonstrating your unreliability," Josh said. Marty waved a flaming piece of wood at Jackie. "Will they know how to put out the campfire?"

Amy heard the disapproval in his voice. "Del security will take care of the fire if they don't. Did it bother you what they said?" Suddenly she wanted to protect him, as if she could.

"No. My job is to defend their right to say whatever stupid things they want. Ignorance comes with the territory. They're young and haven't lived much."

"You sound almost empathetic."

Josh grinned. "Have you forgiven me, then?"

"Getting closer. I need more proof you're genuinely sorry."

Josh faced her. Wavelets rolled almost to their feet. "What can I do?"

"I'll have to think about it," Amy said, surprising herself. "Maybe the next time you run into me I'll have an answer."

"Maybe. How are you getting home tonight?"

"Oh, the time," Amy scrambled for her phone. "You're wearing a watch. I've got to get moving. I've missed the traffic, but it'll take me an hour to drive home through Imperial Beach."

"Listen, can I make up for my big mouth this way?" he asked. "If we leave now, I can drive you and your car over the bridge and then catch a bus back. Will that demonstrate my good intentions? I'll take you back to the other side of the bridge where we started, and you won't have to drive so far?"

"Okay," she said, tilting her head to look at him. "You're definitely on the right track."

Josh laughed. "God's going to get you, Amy. Be prepared."

Chapter 11

He obviously needed to learn a lesson, and Amy felt triumphant she would get the best of him. Funny it took the fear of not being forgiven to get him to admit he was wrong. She'd see him humbled.

As they walked back to the car, Josh whistled the dwarf song from *Snow White*.

"What job are you going off to do now?" she asked.

"Usual job, keeping America safe. In this case, I'm going to drive a foolish woman over a bridge."

"Foolish woman?" She couldn't believe he was insulting her again.

"How long have you known me, Amy? We met four days ago on a bus. What are you thinking letting me get into your car and drive you somewhere? You should be afraid of me, not a concrete piece of road over water."

She stopped and frowned. The scent of sweet jasmine floating on the moist air lulled her for a moment. Lights lined the path, and from Orange Avenue she saw a couple walking in their direction, snuggled together and whispering. Amy felt as safe as that young woman, but his question caused doubt to nibble her soul.

"Have you changed your mind about driving me?" she asked.

"Not at all, but you need to be more careful." He pulled a smartphone from his pocket and tapped on the screen. He turned it in her direction, and she saw a photo of Darlin. "Watch and listen. I'll put the volume on speakerphone."

"Hello!" Amy heard Darlin's energetic voice.

Josh identified himself.

"Where've you been?" Darlin exclaimed. "We thought you were coming to church tonight."

"I'm here with Amy—" He stopped to address her. "What's your last name?"

"Cantrell."

"Amy Cantrell. I escorted her to a gathering at the beach, and I've volunteered to drive her over the bridge to cut down the time she has to be on the road tonight."

"Oh, good idea, but listen, I'm working on—"

Josh broke into her flurry of words. "You can tell me later. Right now I need you to be a character reference. Talk to her." He thrust the phone at Amy.

She heard the curiosity in Darlin's voice when she took the phone. "Can I trust him?" Amy did not take her eyes off Josh.

"Where's he taking you?" Darlin asked, her voice dropped to a warm tease. "Home?"

"Just over the bridge. He's going to catch the bus back from—" she looked her question at Josh.

"Petco Park."

"The baseball stadium." Amy's voice slowed as she watched Josh's expression go blank. Something was making her uneasy, but she didn't think it was fear. Why had he become like an unemotional statue? She pushed the uncertainty aside to pay attention to Darlin.

"I'll tell you what, honey. I'll call you in fifteen minutes.

If you don't answer, I'll assume something has happened, and I'll... What'll I do, Wayne?" Amy heard laughter and then a deep voice in the background.

"Tell Josh, if I don't hear back from you within five minutes of my phone call, I'll send Pete and his friends to find him."

Josh laughed. "Bring 'em on. It might be worth the fun to steal Amy's phone and not answer." He shook his head. "But I won't. We'll call you when we leave the island and give you the fifteen-minute warning."

"It won't take fifteen minutes to get over the bridge. We've got nothing else going on the rest of the evening, so sure. What're you saying, Wayne? Wayne says we're going to bed in an hour, so make it snappy."

"Thank you." Amy returned the phone to its owner, who now looked perfectly normal and engaged. "No guy has ever done that before."

Josh pocketed the phone. "Been accountable?"

Amy felt moisture pool in her eyes. "Something like that. My car is this way."

She noticed he did not walk beside her in the middle of the path, but sort of slinked along the edges of light, almost as if he didn't want to be seen.

"Not every guy is as trustworthy as I am," Josh volunteered.

"Don't I know it," she muttered.

"Do you?" He stopped. "How?"

"If I ever know you longer, and at this moment that's still a big if, I might tell you."

He stuck out his hand. "Deal."

She reached to shake it, and again felt a powerful spark when they touched. She didn't want to let go, but when she looked up and saw the intensity in his eyes, she dropped his hand abruptly.

"I felt it, too," he said.

Amy turned and hurried down the path.

When they reached her battered black Civic parked in the brightly lit parking lot, Josh walked around the car. Amy stowed her backpack in the trunk. "What are you doing now?"

"Habit. I always check out the vehicle I'm riding in. You need two new tires."

Amy groaned. "I know. I'm waiting for my first paycheck to catch up on things."

Josh kicked the right front tire. "If you have to choose, start with this one. May I have your keys?" He opened the passenger door for her. "Shall we go?"

When had someone last opened the door for her? Amy couldn't remember the last time she had sat on the passenger side, either.

When Josh climbed behind the wheel, he took a moment to adjust everything and ask a few questions about how the car operated.

"I thought you were a corpsman," Amy said. "A navy medical guy?"

"Yep."

"Where do you work?"

He turned the key in the ignition. "This week I'll be at Balboa Hospital for training. I'm stationed at NAB."

"You're not telling me something."

He chuckled and turned onto Orange Avenue. "You haven't asked me everything. Call Darlin." He held out his phone.

Amy's roommate Lindsey had a smartphone she'd long admired. She found the contact list and made the call. "Text me your phone number," Darlin replied. "Have fun. He's a nice guy and lonely."

Lonely? Josh hadn't acted lonely tonight with all the people at the beach.

"Why do you work over here?" Josh asked. "Why not work closer to home if you're afraid of the commute?"

"The Del pays a lot more than the athletic department at

San Diego State—which didn't need me during the summer anyway. I've got school loans, and I need to support myself. I took this opportunity for money, but also because it's one of the best spas in the world. I can learn a lot here, if I can manage the drive." Her eyes strayed to the window. She could see the golden lights dotting the black bridge to the east.

"How old are you?"

"Twenty-four. I've had to work my way through school, so I'm a little older than most. Six more classes, though, and I'm done."

"Then what happens?" Josh saluted the church on the corner.

"Why did you salute the church?"

"I like to show respect. It's important to acknowledge the good guys. What will you do when you graduate?"

"I want to go to physical therapy school, but I won't have enough money, so I'll work a couple years and save up," Amy said. "It's not the easiest way, but the whole debt thing worries me."

"Your parents can't help?"

"My mom works for a dentist and does massage on the side. She gets by but needs to put money away for her retirement. She helps where she can." Amy smiled. "She always buys groceries or sends me back with food after I visit, but I can't ask for anything else. She taught me a profession and it's gotten me this far. She prays all the time, which is probably the most important thing."

"She sounds like a great mom." Josh stopped for the light on Fourth Street. "When was the last time you changed your oil?"

"I know how important it is to change the oil," Amy protested. "Look at the sticker in the window."

"You're overdue."

She dropped her head into her hands. Tires, oil, rent, food, gas, it never ended. "I have Monday and Tuesday off, I'll see to it then. I got a good cash tip today."

"I'd buy a new tire first."

Amy felt the car accelerate as they neared the bridge. She tried to fight the nausea rising in her throat. "What kind of car do you have?" All guys liked to talk about their cars, right? Maybe if she paid attention to Josh, she could avoid thinking about the bridge.

"I've got an old Jeep I left with my parents. I don't need a car most of the time. Listen, Amy, there's several ways of dealing with fear. One is to face it and gut it out."

Amy seethed.

"I know that doesn't work for you," Josh continued. "So why not do what I do?"

"What do you do? Demonstrate perfect love to cast out all my fears? You've been just terrific at that."

"I apologized. When I have to do something that unnerves me, I learn all I can about it. Love isn't the only thing that can push back fear; knowledge can do it, too."

Amy wished she hadn't eaten the fatty hot dog. The sour taste in her mouth grew, and she cracked the window open to let in cool air. She would not look up, so she stared at the damp marks her sweaty hands were making on her jeans.

"For example," Josh said, "the civil engineers knew earthquakes happen in California. They built the bridge as safe as possible. It's not going anywhere, even if a big ship like a cargo tanker or even an aircraft carrier hit it."

"Why are you telling me this?" Amy could barely speak through her gritted teeth.

"I've been in dangerous places in my time, and this bridge is nothing like them. I'm trying to point out how safe you really are. You don't have to worry about cars flying through intersections and T-boning you, kids running out in the street and getting hit when you're on a bridge. It's a smooth long stretch where all you have to do is steer. Piece of cake."

"I hate you."

"No you don't," Josh said. "We're over. Petco Park's ahead and I'll get out."

"You did that on purpose, didn't you?"

He drove without speaking and pulled to the side of the road when he saw a bus stop. "Darlin should be calling soon. I'll be gone." Josh put the car into Park, set the brake, and got out. "Are we square yet?"

Amy opened her mouth to speak, but the phone rang. She hardly knew how to answer Darlin's sparkling question: "Are you still safe?"

Josh walked away.

Chapter 12

"Where were you last night?" Pete sat in the recliner turning the pages of the Sunday *San Diego Union Tribune* newspaper.

"I drove Amy over the bridge then wandered around in the Gaslight Quarter before catching a bus back."

Pete's eyebrows went up. "Amy? That girl on the bus? What's she like?"

"Feisty. You coming to church this morning?"

"I'm ready when you are." Pete released the chair, and they headed out the door together.

Tourists flocked to Coronado Island on Sunday mornings in June. Cars laden with beachgoers cluttered Orange Avenue, and residents came out in force to play. Josh probably saw more people walking to church that morning than he saw in a month while growing up in Boonville.

Joggers ran by in abbreviated shorts, and dog walkers took to the streets. The tall palm tree fronds waved gently in the off-shore breezes, and a general spirit of happiness infused the air. Josh was happy, too. He hadn't been to church in a month and looked forward to singing and hearing a good sermon.

They arrived fifteen minutes early and stopped to greet people they recognized. Darlin hadn't climbed onto the organ bench yet, and she squealed when she saw Pete. "So good to see you again."

"Hey there, Darlin. You need to get a choir going. I always told my mama if there was a choir, I'd be in church."

"Wayne," Darlin called across the sanctuary. "We need to start a choir so Pete here will make it to church more often."

Pastor Wayne shook Pete's hand. "I'll start one if you'll run it."

"Sorry, sir. No guarantees of when I'll be here."

"That's what I figured. What's your favorite hymn? We'll slip it in to keep you interested."

Pete grinned. " 'Great Is Thy Faithfulness.' "

"You hear that, Darlin? Stick it in the lineup."

"My pleasure." Darlin took to the keys.

Josh preferred the praise music he'd grown up with, but Pete listened with a bemused expression on his face. "She's very good."

"Don't let her hear you say that. It will go to her head."

A shout of laughter, a quick run up the scale, and Darlin swung into "Great is Thy Faithfulness."

They walked to the third pew on the right and sat down.

Pete thought better of the choice. "We never sit with our backs to the door."

"If I die in church, I go straight to heaven," Josh said. "Bring 'em on."

"Yeah, great, and I'll have to explain to Chief."

The Community Church had been on the island for over a hundred years and featured a cross section of Coronado life, ranging from the young children of military personnel through Carlos and other firemen, various middle-aged shop owners, and a handful of elderly people who claimed their antique wooden pews with vigor. Mrs. Martin, who always sat in the front row right side, had been baptized in the church and proudly told anyone in hearing distance that her grandfather had been a member of the original building committee.

Josh liked her and always gave her his best salute when they met. Her aviator husband had piloted all sorts of planes through World War II, Korea, and Vietnam and been known as a sailor's admiral. She cackled and waved her cane, but he doubted she knew his name or much else about him.

All of which was just as well.

You shouldn't really keep a low profile at church, but in his line of business it was better if people didn't know much about him. Josh ran his hand across his forehead and sighed. At least he didn't have to pretend to be anything but who he was with God. For ninety minutes he could feel known, forgiven, and loved.

Pete looked thoughtful after Pastor Wayne pronounced the benediction. "Don't be afraid of those who can kill the body but not the soul," he repeated. "What do you make of that, Josh?"

"What the pastor said. It's more important to make sure your heart is right with God than to be afraid of what another person can do to you."

"Is that what you think about when you meet up with the bad guys?" Josh could barely hear Pete's words.

"That's what I think of before I meet the bad guys. I need to stay focused on the mission when I'm in the middle of it."

"Absolutely." They bumped knuckles.

Josh waited for Mrs. Martin to hobble up the aisle. In a formidable red hat that probably cost more than he made in a month, she trod carefully down the forest-green carpet runner that ran from the front door all the way to the altar. She looked up at him from under the brim with pursed lips. He thrust back his shoulders and snapped a smart salute.

"Thank you." As the double doors opened, a whoosh of air blew down the aisle and the chiffon sleeves of her purple dress billowed like the vestments of a queen. She teetered a moment on her scarlet high-heeled shoes and then regained her balance.

On impulse, Josh stuck out his elbow, and she grasped it. "You will do nicely for an escort, though I prefer a man in uniform."

"She flirts with every man who lets her," said her daughter Susan, who followed after carrying her mother's purse.

They walked out together.

Josh lifted his head. Was that Amy slipping out the back?

Mrs. Martin dropped the crook of his arm when they stepped into the bright sunlight and shook hands with Pastor Wayne and Darlin.

Mrs. Martin had a last word. "You did a fine job, young man. You may have a future in the military."

"Thank you, ma'am."

Darlin chatted with Mrs. Martin's daughter. "You just missed her, Susan." Darlin's diamond ring flashed as she waved her hands. "I'll text you her phone number. I'm praying it all works out."

Darlin beamed at Josh. "I think it's going to come together."

"What's that?"

"You'll find out. Keep praying." She took Pete's hand. "Call in your requests any time. Because of you, I got to play my favorite hymn today."

"They're all your favorite hymns," Pastor Wayne protested. "You can play whatever you want whenever you want."

"A girl's got to have mystery, Wayne. Don't give away my secrets." She leaned forward toward Josh. "I'm not playing next week. It's a praise service, so make sure you come back."

"I'll do my best."

Pete thumbed over his shoulder. "Let's go to lunch at McP's."

"On a day like this?" Josh said. "Why sit in a dark pub

when we can be out in the sunshine? I'm ready to go surfing or take a run."

"Team meeting. We can probably sit outside if we get there early."

"On Sunday?" Josh protested.

"Chief's got tickets to the baseball game tonight. You need to check in."

Josh wanted to argue, but came up with a better question. "What time's the game?"

"Doesn't it usually start at seven?"

"Perfect."

They walked down the street to the SEAL team's favorite pub, McP's, on the Orange Avenue corner and not far from the Hotel Del. Josh and Pete ordered Cokes, grabbed menus, and headed for the patio enclosed by a chest-high adobe wall. Tarzan and his ten-year-old son sat at a large table under an umbrella. Flip sat beside them, gazing into space.

"We're out here because I've got the kid with me," Tarzan growled.

"It's a great day to be outside. I heard you've become a Boy Scout, Tyler." Josh sat beside the boy. His red hair and freckled face, not to mention his age, set him apart from the rest of the pub patrons.

The boy stared at a Nintendo screen. "Yeah. It's cool."

"Been camping yet?"

"No." Tyler glanced at his father. "It's best with dads."

"I finally come home and can sleep in a bed, and the kid wants me to grab my sleeping bag." Tarzan's eyes turned to slits. "That'll be the day."

Josh turned back to the boy. "Where does your troop like to camp?"

Tyler shrugged. "They're talking about going out to the islands."

"I want a house burger and fries," Pete said. "Why don't you go find what happened to our waitress, Josh?"

Josh went into the pub. One of his team members followed him. "Go easy on the kid. Be careful what you say. Don't give him any false hopes."

"What do you mean?"

"Didn't you see how tight Tarzan got? You rub him the wrong way too many times and I'm afraid he'll blow."

Josh frowned. "I'm not afraid of Tarzan."

"A word to the wise: watch what you say."

While Josh waited at the bar to give his order, a guy he knew from another team reached around him to grab a toothpick. "You want to angel up?"

"Sure. When?" Josh watched the TV screen and barely moved his lips.

"Four weeks. Watch for a text. In the bay or out?"

"Wherever you need me."

"Thanks." The guy stuck the toothpick in his mouth, picked up his drink, and disappeared.

When Josh returned with their food, half the sixteen-man platoon had gathered in the courtyard. Chief hoisted his tankard. "We're on for the game tonight, tickets for everyone from a supporter. Since you've got your kid, Tarzan, can you be the designated driver? I assume you'll volunteer to do the same, Cubby."

"Cubby's got a kid? How did that happen?" One of the team jokers punched him.

"I'll come late, but if someone will drive a van over, I'll meet you at the game and drive everyone back." Josh took a bite out of his hamburger.

Chief frowned. "What do you mean you'll come late?"

Josh swallowed. "I'll be there by the eighth inning, maybe earlier. It depends."

Pete raised his eyebrows and reached for his food. "You got a hot date?"

Josh grinned. "Maybe I do."

Chapter 13

Amy should not have been surprised when she pushed out of the glass spa doors and saw Josh sitting on the wall again, but she was. Flattered, too, but also peeved. Now what was she supposed to do? Forgive him?

"I don't think so," she said aloud.

He hopped off the wall. "Are you going to forgive me yet?"

"Is this genuine repentance?" she asked. "Why is your hair wet?"

"It's a beautiful day, I practiced my high dive. I've come as a penitent. I need a favor."

She closed her eyes. Those white teeth against his healthy good looks and gorgeous eyes. She needed to think without the distraction of seeing him. "What is it?"

"I need a ride to Petco Park. Can you help me?"

Amy opened one eye. "You want to ride with me all the way through Imperial Beach to get to the park? You caught a bus home last night without any problem. What gives?"

He held out a single stem carnation that she had not noticed before. "Not exactly. I see this as a win-win. I'll drive your car across the bridge to the park, get out, and you can go home. How long did it take you to get home last night?"

It bugged her to have to admit it. "Twenty minutes."

"What was your commute this morning coming in?" He offered the carnation again. She ignored it.

"It's summertime, so Silver Strand was crowded. I left early."

"Do you want this flower? How long?"

"Where did you get the flower?"

"I stole it, of course. What do you think? Did I see you in church?"

Amy gasped. "Church. I forgot. I have an appointment at your church at six thirty. What time is it?"

He checked his watch. "It's 6:05. I'll walk over there with you while you think up a reason not to ride across the bridge with me."

"That's not fair. But you're right. I'm being rude." Amy brushed the hair off her forehead. "It took me ninety minutes to drive around. After you pointed out my tire last night, I went online and googled tire bulge." She frowned and stalked down the sidewalk.

Josh trailed behind. "What did you learn?"

"It's dangerous to drive with a bulging tire. I need a new one soon. I'll buy one tomorrow, but I was afraid to drive very fast, so it took forever to drive around the bay. I was so worried I left at nine o'clock. Then I got here too early to go to work but too late to attend your church. I decided to go anyway and sat in the back, but then I had to hurry out to make it to work on time. What a crazy day."

Josh broke off the carnation stem and stuck the flower behind her ear. "My mom always said flowers perk up the craziest day."

"Really?"

He shrugged. "Sure."

She stopped in her tracks. "Are you deliberately trying to be a man of mystery? Can I believe anything you say?"

The merriment fled from Josh's face, and he went blank. Amy stepped back in surprise.

"I beg your pardon. Have you got a date? Am I intruding?" he asked.

She was tempted to say yes, but that wasn't exactly true. "Are you ready to change?"

"Maybe. Listen, I thought this would solve your problem and mine for at least one night. I'll find a different way to the park. See you another time."

"No, Josh." Amy's heart sank. "I'm meeting a woman about a room on Coronado in exchange for minor help. It shouldn't take more than half an hour. If you'll wait, I'd appreciate a drive across the bridge."

His look pierced her, and she caught her breath. "I'll pray while I wait for you," he said.

"Thank you."

Darlin's hands fluttered when Amy entered the church library. "I believe you met Mrs. Martin and her daughter, Susan Armstrong, yesterday. Susan's been looking for someone to do respite care for her mother, and I thought of you."

Amy shook hands with Mrs. Martin, who sat with a straight back in the upholstered chair, her knees tight together and her ankles neatly crossed.

"I'm so glad to see you again," Amy said. "Thank you for thinking of me."

"I'm not convinced I need a night nurse, but Susan tells me it will make her sleep better, so here I am."

"We've been through this, Mother. Having someone in the house is a precaution, nothing more." Susan's eyes flashed, but Amy recognized weariness in her determined features. Susan needed a massage.

"How can I help you, Mrs. Armstrong? What would the arrangement be?"

While her mother spoke with a pointed charm, Susan's words marched like numbers across a spreadsheet. "Call me Susan. Mother has a companion during the day who fixes her dinner and leaves about seven o'clock when the dishes are finished. I need you to make sure Mother is settled in bed about nine thirty."

"Eleven o'clock," Mrs. Martin said.

Susan glared at her. "Whenever Mother wants to go to bed. If you're in by nine thirty that probably would work. Make breakfast for her in the morning, see to any minor chores around the house, and you're done. She can dress herself."

"I've been doing it for eighty-six years." Mrs. Martin didn't exactly growl, but Amy heard her irritation. "Coffee, toast, and fruit is all I really eat. One of us is trying to keep her figure in check."

Susan folded her hands. "Ella usually comes about ten and manages the household. She and Mother run errands together. I'm not sure you'd ever actually see her, but I'd expect you to keep her and me informed of anything we need to know."

"Spies."

"Mother. It's this or you know what."

Mrs. Martin picked up her cane, thumped it on the floor, and then swiveled her head to examine the children's books on the nearby shelf.

"I would basically be on call for any needs Mrs. Martin might have in the night, is that correct?" Amy said. "No cleaning, no personal care, only making breakfast and that's it? Would I have my own room? How much would you charge, and would I have kitchen privileges?"

"Well," Susan began.

Another cane thump. "Don't be ridiculous," Mrs. Martin said to Susan before facing Amy. "You'll be down the hall from me since one of Susan's worries is I'll fall out of bed at night. As if that would ever happen. Your own room, your own bath, we'll share the kitchen; you may eat any food you like, and if this is satisfactory to you, no charge at all. I may need extra foot massages."

Amy's mouth dropped open and tears prickled her eyes. She blinked rapidly. No rent? Her hopes soared. Her practical mind argued there had to be a catch. She reined in her emotions. "What if I don't suit your needs? How many nights a week?"

"Do you have somewhere else to sleep?" Mrs. Martin asked.

Amy's left hand rubbed her right as the three women watched her. "This is generous and so much beyond anything I dreamed. But if I agree to this, I will give up my apartment for the summer. If you don't like me or it doesn't work out, I won't have a place to go. I'm a single young woman. I can't take the risk to my reputation or my job at the Del if I'm suddenly homeless."

She bowed her head and heard the clock ticking on the wall. The rustle in the room told her the women were reacting to her words. Her head spun, and she prayed she had not thrown away her opportunity.

Darlin took her hand. "Let's pray and start over. Give us wisdom, Lord, amen."

"Tell us what we need to know about you, Amy," Susan said. "I should have started there."

"Where are your parents?" Mrs. Martin asked.

"I grew up in San Pedro, the port of Los Angeles, across the street from Trinity Lutheran Church, which is where I've always worshipped. My mother works as a receptionist in the dentist office. She does massage on the side, which is where I first learned how to take care of clients. I'm an only child without any relatives. I don't have a boyfriend, and I'm self-supporting. Like I told you yesterday, when I graduate I want to go to physical therapy school."

"Where's your father?" Mrs. Martin asked.

Amy closed her eyes briefly then faced Mrs. Martin. "My

parents divorced when I was a little girl. He's a teacher and lives near Sacramento with his wife and a bunch of kids. I haven't seen him nor received any money from him since I graduated from high school. It's only Mom and me."

"Oh, honey," Darlin began.

Amy interrupted. "He wasn't much of a father anyway, and Mom and I learned early on to trust God to take care of us. Dad wasn't available." It was an old wound, but every time she thought she was past the hurt, a stab occurred. "That's why I have to be careful. There's not much margin for trouble in my life."

She thought of her tire. Not much at all.

"Is your Del job only a summer slot?" Susan asked.

A reasonable and good question. "I don't know what will happen at the Del, but they know I'm a student going back to school in September. It would be wonderful if I could continue here, but the bridge is a problem for me."

"Very well," Mrs. Martin said. "I'll take you on for the summer, unless, of course, either one of us has moral flaws the other can't live with. Then you'd have to go. When can you move in?"

Amy smiled in relief. This would make such a difference for her peace of mind. She'd make it work, no matter what she had to do. "I have Mondays and Tuesdays off and chores to do tomorrow. I'll be there no later than Tuesday. Where do you live?"

Chapter 14

Amy moved in a daze as she left the church, but a smile twisted at her lips. Behind her, Darlin beamed and gave Josh a thumbs-up.

"What happened?" Josh asked.

"I've been offered a place to live on Coronado," Amy said. "I can't believe it."

"Great. Where?"

She handed him a piece of paper with a scribbled address. "It's Mrs. Martin. Do you know where this is?"

He nodded. Everyone on Coronado knew the house. "We'll swing by there on our way over the bridge. You're probably hungry, though. Want to get something to eat first?"

"I'm starved, but don't you have to get to the game?" They started walking back to the Del.

"As long as I'm there by the eighth inning, they'll be happy. I'm the designated driver. You like Greek food? I'll take you to a great gyro spot I know not far from where you'll be living."

"Only if I can pay my own way," Amy said.

"Of course. This is a business arrangement."

When they got to her car, Josh dropped to his heels to examine the tire. "Have you got a spare? Why don't I put that on so you don't have to worry about this one?"

"I've got an appointment first thing tomorrow morning at a tire shop near my house. I told you I would take care of it."

Josh pushed at the soft bulge. He didn't like it. "I would feel better if I could change it now."

"Then the tire people would have to swap both my spare and my front tire and that's more money."

"I'll give you the ten bucks."

"I'm about to rescind my agreement to a ride." She crossed her arms and stuck out her chin.

He held out his hand. "Your keys."

Mrs. Martin lived up by the North Island Navy Base. He knew her house because he often admired it while kayaking on the bay. She had one of the few privately owned waterfronts that faced downtown San Diego, not far from the ferry landing.

"Oh, my," Amy said when he stopped the car on the street opposite her driveway. The house hid behind two pillared gates and shrubbery, but they could see the roofline from the street and the width of the lot. "I figured she was wealthy when she told me her family had owned property on the island for over a hundred years."

"You'll do fine with her as long as you are an honorable and trustworthy woman," Josh said.

She nodded. "I'm not brave, and I can't make a fire, but I have lots of Boy Scout traits."

He laughed. "No, you don't. I know Boy Scouts."

"Why did she choose me?"

"What did she say?"

"The two hours I spent with her yesterday made her think we could get along. I genuinely liked her, and I think the massage helped," Amy said. "Do you suppose she'll want a massage every day?"

"Would that be too much to ask?"

"Only on days when I'm tired. I hope this works. It will make my life so much easier."

"Then we'll pray it will." Josh started the car and pulled onto the street. He didn't like the way the car drove but couldn't tell if he actually felt something, or if it was his knowledge of the soft spot on the tire that made the ride feel so tentative. He took it easy while Amy looked out the window at her new neighborhood. With the sun going down, streetlights glowed, as did the city across the water.

They bought gyros and sat outside to enjoy the view and the tranquil evening from near the ferry dock. Josh preferred to visit this restaurant in the evening when the pigeons roosted elsewhere and the tourists went home. He sipped his drink and watched Amy devour her hummus. "I like to see a girl enjoy her food."

"I'm starving. I did four massages today. That's the max." Amy shook her arms and rotated her shoulders. "I'm glad I've got two days off. I need them."

"It's nice to have a weekend off. Most of the time our training goes through the weekends. That's why we've mastered the technique of sleeping anywhere."

"I thought you worked in a hospital."

"I'll be at the hospital this week. That'll be fun."

"Fun? I don't understand your job."

"No need to. Listen, I did some research today on the Internet, and I'd like to talk to you about it. Will you promise not to get angry?"

"What sort of research?"

"Fear of bridges. It's called gephyrophobia."

Amy slumped on the bench. "Aren't you afraid of anything?"

"Sure." He laughed. "I'm afraid of all the same things people fear: clowns, spiders, and things that go bump in the night."

"I'm serious. Doesn't anything make you go cold all over and want to scream?"

"Nosey girls? Paparazzi? Intrusive newspaper reporters? That's it. I'm afraid of reporters." He leaned back in the chair and grinned at her. Her cheeks were turning red, and she bit her lip. Maybe he had pushed her too far.

"I don't know why I even bother to talk to you. You don't get it." Amy wiped her mouth with a paper napkin and stared at her food.

Josh narrowed his eyes. "I'm a logical person. I evaluate the odds and the risk. I work hard in my job to make sure those risks are minimized so I don't have to be afraid. I reason my way through anything that makes me feel uneasy."

Her left hand went over her right hand and rubbed in a smooth, round pattern.

He pointed to her hands. "Does that help?"

"What?"

"Rubbing your hands like that. I've seen you do it before."

Her movement slowed. "I suppose so. It grounds me and reminds me what is real."

Josh sipped his drink and watched her sitting with her legs crossed and her elbows close to her body as if she was protecting herself from something. He probably was the reason for her nerves, but he wasn't sure why. Would confessing a fear make her like him better? Did he care? He'd try.

"Pastor Wayne preached on fear once and gave us an acronym: *F* stands for false; *E* for evidence; *A* for appearing; and *R* for real. Fear is no more than false evidence appearing real to the individual. The acronym helps me evaluate a situation: What do I fear, and is it a real fear?"

"You don't believe I'm afraid of the bridge?" she asked in a limp voice.

"I'm convinced you're scared to death of the bridge, though I wonder why. Is it only the Coronado Bridge or can you drive over other bridges? This one is just a beam bridge, no cables or trusses. Is that part of the problem?"

"I've never driven over a bridge," Amy said.

"Never? Not once?"

She shook her head and golden curls bounced around her ears.

"Does it matter what type of bridge it is?" Josh pulled a piece of paper from his pocket. "I looked up facts about our local monster. The Coronado Bridge is a little over two miles long, goes two hundred feet up in the air and is high enough for commercial tankers to go under."

He didn't tell her it was the third deadliest suicide bridge in the country.

Amy sat with her back to the bridge, not even looking over her shoulder. Facing her, Josh watched a stream of car lights buzz up the incline and follow the bridge's bend to the left toward the tall buildings of downtown San Diego. The sun's dying rays had completely disappeared, and the blue waters of the bay rustled incessantly.

"I don't know why I get so scared," she said. "I nearly killed myself coming over for the interview at the Hotel Del. I kept thinking I could do it. I just needed to look straight ahead and not panic. It's just a road. I even prayed for peace and safety before I left my apartment."

"What happened?" Josh noticed her hands were moving again.

"I was fine until I got over the water; you know where the bridge starts to angle up? And then I started shaking, my eyes got blurry, and I couldn't see. A big truck rattled by too close on the left, I braked and skidded, and the next thing I knew the car stopped along the waterside barrier. I was crying so hard, I couldn't see."

"Were you hurt? Was your car damaged?"

She shook her head. "I didn't know what to do, so I sat there until a police car stopped with two officers."

Josh frowned. This story sounded familiar.

"I shook so badly, one of the officers drove my car over the bridge. I couldn't have made it without him. Then they threatened to cite me for not having an operating right turn light."

"I guess it could have been worse. Did they ticket you?" Josh asked.

"No, but they told me I needed to get the light fixed before leaving Coronado. Fortunately, my Civic only had a dead light bulb. I replaced it, had the interview, and drove home the long way."

"I grew up traveling over the Golden Gate Bridge," Josh said, "so I'm surprised people never cross water. Where did you grow up?"

"San Pedro. There's a suspension bridge near my hometown, the Vincent Thomas Bridge, over the harbor to Long Beach. I haven't traveled over it since I was a little girl. I panic just thinking about it."

"Did something bad happen on the bridge?"

Her face went white and her hands stilled. Josh waited.

"I don't remember," Amy finally said. "What time is it? I'm sure we need to go."

People chatted and laughed freely around them. Folks came and went to the ferry, children called for their mothers and couples paused for a tight embrace. Here at the table, however, Josh recognized spine-tingling fear.

"Listen, Amy, everyone is afraid of something. Being scared isn't a character flaw. What's important is what you do with your fear. Face it, admit it, figure out why it bothers you and either avoid it or deal with it. I can see you're trying. I'll be praying for you."

Her reply came through tight lips. "Thank you. How can I pray for you since you have no fears?"

Chief's face and Tarzan's scowl flashed in his mind. "Pray I learn to keep my mouth shut. As you know, I stick my foot in it all the time."

Amy wore the tiniest smile as she gathered up her purse. "But you're getting lots of practice in apologizing."

He thought of a retort, but managed to refrain. Making mistakes and causing problems with the team were unacceptable in his job.

Josh escorted her to the car and unlocked the door. He glanced at the front of the car; it looked lower. "I'd really like to put on the spare."

Amy trembled. "Please, can we just go?"

He took it slow and easy. The 1995 Honda and its owner would both need to be nursed over the bridge.

Chapter 15

Amy took deep breaths and willed herself to relax as they drove under the abandoned canopy, passed the U-turn area, and then climbed up the bridge. She envisioned each of the muscles in her body, starting at her face, and deliberately tried to make them slack.

She turned away from Josh so he couldn't see how ridiculous she looked with her mouth hanging open, and then she slumped her shoulders. Even the newest massage therapists knew hunched shoulders signified tension.

Amy leaned forward in her seat and dangled her hands toward the floor to relieve muscle tension in her back. She consciously unclenched the muscles in her legs. By focusing on relaxation rather than the bridge, she might make it over.

Josh adjusted the mirror several times. "What's this guy's problem?"

"What's wrong?"

"It's hard to baby the car when somebody's riding your tail."

"Speed up. The sooner we're over the bridge, the better."

Out the window she saw the sparkling lights of the cruise docks and the line of yellow glare marking the convention center along the water. Amy tried to swallow the knot threatening her breathing. She could tell when they reached the highest part of the bridge and swallowed to relieve the air pressure in her ears.

Just after the road turned to the left on its bend back to earth, she heard a loud bang near her right ear. The car tilted, a whoosh, *thunk, thunk, thunk*.

She screamed. "Do something!"

Josh held the car with rigid arms and the veins stuck out of his neck. "Come on, baby, you can do it."

The car sped up. "Hit the brakes," Amy shrieked.

All sense of relaxation fled, her muscles were rigid with fear, and she braced herself against the dashboard. The car slid to the right with the acrid smell of burning rubber filling the car. Josh turned the wheel to the left.

Bam, bam, bam.

Amy's teeth hurt from the vibration. Time slowed and San Diego's bright lights revolved before her eyes. She shut them tight and shielded her head with her arms.

The car slalomed all over the road, slowed, and then stopped.

Silence.

The taste of burned rubber reached her mouth and nose.

Her cramped fingers ached.

Amy opened her eyes.

Josh leaned on the steering wheel looking right at her. "Can I change the tire now?"

A man knocked on her window. Amy rolled it down. "You okay? What happened? Blown tire?"

"Yeah," Josh said. "Is it safe to get out?"

"Yes. My wife's calling the CHP. Man, you were all over the road. I've never seen driving like it, how did you keep control?"

Josh flicked on the emergency flashers and got out of the car. "I've been through it before."

She couldn't look at him. This was her fault. Amy put her face in her hands and wept.

With two California Highway Patrol officers managing traffic, Josh safely put on the spare tire. "You're going to have to replace this rim, but it's a small price to pay," he said to her.

She stood beside him, her arms as tight across her chest as she could get them. She felt numb and unnerved to the very bone. Amy could hardly speak and didn't dare glance over the three-foot-high concrete barrier that had kept them from going into the water forty feet below.

"You okay, ma'am?" one patrolman asked. "It could happen to anyone. You're lucky you were with a good driver."

Amy nodded.

He turned to Josh. "I followed your skid mark. You did a terrific job. You say you've been through this before?"

Josh lifted the tire effortlessly into the trunk. Amy noted his shirt was greasy from changing the tire. She'd wash it for him. She'd kiss his feet. She'd never speak to him again. Humiliation flooded and rivaled the terror. All she wanted was to curl up and never leave home again.

His words with the officer barely sank in.

"I've taken advanced driving courses with the military. I've practiced maneuvers like this before."

"I figured you were a SEAL. Good job. Think you can get her home now?"

"I'm not sure. I'm supposed to pick up some guys at Petco Park as the designated driver. Any idea what the score is on the game and what inning they're in?"

"We'll find it." He walked back to the patrol car.

"I'm so cold," Amy said when Josh stopped beside her.

"I'm dirty, but I'd be happy to hug you if you think it will help."

She turned against his hard chest and leaned in. He

wrapped his arms around her, and she felt his strong warmth. "Father God, thank You for saving us from serious injury tonight. I pray You'd calm Amy's heart and get her home safely. Thank You for Your love. Amen."

"Amen," she whispered. She nestled as close as she could get to his hard chest, his warmth, his strength and felt her knees wobble.

"Hey," he said. "Let's sit you down and put your head between your knees. You've had a shock."

He slid down the cement barrier with her and forced her head between her knees. She gulped at the air, smelled the burned rubber all over again, gagged, and coughed. "I can't breathe."

"Back on your feet." He reached into the car. "Put on your jacket. You need to stay warm."

Josh walked her to the back end of the car and leaned her against the trunk while he helped her with the jacket. He put his arms around her again. "Breathe slowly, steadily, and carefully with me."

Vaguely she heard the highway patrolman return. "Does she need medical help?"

"She's reacting to the shock. I'm a corpsman. She'll be fine as soon as she gets home. What's the score?"

"Top of the fifth. Where do you live?"

"I'm on Coronado. Amy lives near San Diego State. I'll drive her home and catch a cab back for the end of the game. We better get moving."

"We'll follow you a ways to make sure the car is sound."

"Thanks, officers." Josh helped her back into the car and turned on the heat. "How do I get to your house?"

Amy roused herself enough to ask a question. "Will the car work?"

"I think so, but have the mechanic check when you get the new tire tomorrow. Let's go."

With the heat blasting and his calm steady voice talking,

Amy directed him to her apartment. The lights were on when they arrived and Josh helped her up the stairs. Before she got the key in the door, it opened and Lindsey burst out. "Hey, you're in time for pizza. Amy? What happened?"

"Josh will explain." She burst into tears and ran to the bathroom where she lost her dinner. Sliding to the floor in misery, she sobbed.

Chapter 16

Even though Josh would be training at the navy's medical center in Balboa Park most of the week, he still had to participate in morning physical training. PT started at 0500, five in the morning, for him and several others. They ran the beach past the BUD/S trainees, went through the obstacle course, zipped across the street, and swam for half an hour before changing into clean uniforms.

Josh drove Pete's Camaro and left for Balboa at seven fifteen. He roared onto the bridge and hit fifty miles per hour in seconds. It felt good to power the car, especially after last night's disaster. As he reached the top and the curve toward downtown San Diego, he could see burn marks on the cement roadway. Josh slowed and frowned.

Pieces of the blown tire littered the area along the side rail. Burned rubber marks veered to the right on the road—he remembered that clearly—and then straightened to the left. His forearms ached from how hard he'd clenched the wheel trying to maintain control. If his stomach hadn't been turning flips at the moment, Josh would have felt smug. His instructors had taught him well. He hadn't hit the center divider nor even rubbed the side of the car against the guardrail.

Of course, Josh had trained in different circumstances, not on a narrow bridge, but the first few times he had a tire shot out from under him had been unnerving. Living through it six times and being evaluated on his reaction meant he'd gone through a lot of tires, but he had known instinctively what to do when Amy's tire blew.

"I told her last night," he said aloud. "One of the best ways to deal with fear is to gain knowledge and practice."

Of course you had to be in a peculiar line of work to practice such skills.

He rubbed the sore left side of his neck. Nausea flared and he shivered. No wonder Amy feared the bridge. They had come close to disaster last night. If there had been any other car on the road near them, they might not have walked away.

As he drove past where he'd changed the tire, Josh thought of Amy sobbing against his chest and how he'd tried to comfort her. His parents had taught him to care for people in distress, whether they deserved it or not.

It served her right to be scared. She should have let him change the tire. He hoped she'd learned her lesson.

Maybe now she'd forgive him? He'd make her eat crow.

If he didn't have to eat some himself—it disturbed him to drive past the spot.

Josh turned off his smartphone as he entered one of the hospital training rooms half an hour later. New protocols for wound care in the field, assessment skills, and the annual refresher CPR training were on the docket. While Josh knew the basic plan behind the upcoming team training cycle, surprise medical training always made him suspicious.

He didn't turn his phone on until he got back home at dinnertime with Pete's burrito and several bags of groceries. The TV blared a baseball game. Josh handed him the fast food.

"How'd the road warrior do today?" Pete pulled his dinner from the white paper bag.

"No problems. What happened with the team?"

"They scored you an eight based on your skid marks." Pete grinned. "We took a field trip out to admire your work after the CHP called the command and asked where you went to driver's safety school. I guess they don't run into successful stunt drivers every day."

"No stunt. Amy was stupid and wouldn't let me change the tire, even though I volunteered three times."

Pete put up his hands. "Don't get mad at me."

"She's a walking disaster." He shook his head. "It's pretty pathetic when you feel safer at SEAL training than driving a girl's car."

"A pretty girl can do that to you. You going to drive her across every night?" Pete snickered and took a bite of the fat burrito with everything in it.

He shook his head. "She's beautiful, but I could never be with someone who won't face her fears."

Josh scrolled through the messages on his phone. He really needed to call his folks. An unidentified person had left a message. He held down the number one on his touch pad and waited. When the message began, his abs clenched at the sound of her breathless voice.

"Hi, Josh, this is Amy. Amy Cantrell. I've called to thank you for saving my life last night and to apologize for not letting you change the tire. I'm so ashamed. I put your life at risk and that was wrong. I'm so sorry. Thank you and I won't bother you again. Good-bye."

A pause, and then she whispered a hurried remark. "One more thing, I forgive you. Bye."

Josh looked at the female silhouette on the smartphone's screen. He shrugged. He might want her phone number again, so he saved it to his contacts list. He might even get around to forgiving her someday.

Josh pushed at the sore muscles in his neck and then pulled the groceries from the shopping bags to stow away. He deserved a good meal and planned to barbeque a steak and corn on the cob.

Pete peered into a bag. "All I got was a burrito?"

"There's ice cream for dessert." Josh stepped onto the porch and sloshed lighter fluid over the briquettes in the hibachi.

Pete rubbed his hands together. "Perfect for a Coronado summer's evening. I'm glad you're around to share it with me, Cubby."

Josh laughed. "I'm not easy to kill."

"We're not done trying yet. New orders came today. We're headed to San Clemente Island Friday morning to play the bad guys for a couple weeks."

The tire dealer whistled when he saw the remains of Amy's blown tire and marveled when he found nothing seriously damaged on her car. When she described the event, he rocked back in surprise. "You're lucky you had a race car driver behind the wheel."

"He said he was a navy corpsman," she said. "But the highway patrolman thought he was a SEAL."

"One of those guys who can save your life or kill you with his bare hands? He obviously knew what to do in an emergency. Your blowout could have been serious, especially on that dangerous bridge."

Amy knew.

Josh had saved her life without asking for anything in return. Most guys Amy had dealt with in the past were not so generous. How would she ever repay him?

Amy rang the bell beside Mrs. Martin's driveway gate at four o'clock Tuesday afternoon and drove into the driveway when it swung open. She had all the important things she needed in her car, which was now wearing two new front tires. Lindsey would bring the rest of her possessions on Friday afternoon when she joined Amy for Bible study. After Sunday night's accident, Amy felt a renewed gratitude to God for His protection.

Living on Coronado, she could park her car and not have to worry about driving over a bridge, paying for gas, or even dealing with tires. Mrs. Martin and God had given her a fabulous gift, and she was going to make the most of it. Not having to pay rent meant she could save even more money for school next year. She had one less thing to worry about.

Susan met Amy at the door of the sprawling modern home and led her through a wide foyer directly into the living room, which faced the water. Amy gasped as she saw all of San Diego spread out before her. Off to the right, the Coronado ferry chugged to its dock. To the left, an aircraft carrier filled the view.

Mrs. Martin wore boating clothes—a blue-and-white horizontal-striped shirt over white slacks and a bright red sweater to match her lipstick. She sat in a regal wicker chair on the patio, and Amy had to stifle an urge to kneel before her.

"Did you have any problems finding the house?" Mrs. Martin asked.

"No. I drove through Imperial Beach and am glad I won't have to worry about the bridge until I leave. Thank you for taking me in."

"You're welcome. Susan will show you to your room. Make yourself at home."

Susan helped Amy carry her luggage into the comfortable room at the front of the house facing the driveway, down the hall from Susan's room and the lavish master suite facing the water where Mrs. Martin slept. The room boasted a walk-in closet and a private bathroom. Amy had never had either before. Excited, she pinched her arms to convince herself she actually lived in such a showplace.

Susan showed her around the house and they ended in

the gleaming kitchen, where she explained how things operated and by whom. A notebook kept on the counter listed phone numbers and information pertinent to the house and to Mrs. Martin. Everything was in order, and Amy hugged herself joyfully.

They ate outside on the patio where they could watch the sky fade to mauve and the lights of San Diego twinkle to life. Amy could see people riding the ferry, sailing on their boats, taking down the flag on the aircraft carrier—but they were small and insignificant.

High walls shielded them from whatever was on the other side. Few sounds beyond the splashing water and a sea bird's shrill call reached them. Cocooned by tall hedges, all Amy saw was the modern house, the patio, green lawn to the water, and then the magnificent view.

Susan left precisely at seven. Amy and Mrs. Martin remained on the patio as the sky darkened and finally turned to black. "You don't need to entertain me," Mrs. Martin said, "but I'm happy for the company. I have been watching this view my whole life, and I never grow weary of it."

"I can see why. A lot has probably changed since you were a girl."

"Indeed. Only the water, the sky, and the property remain the same. I savor it all." She motioned to the house. "This is not the home I grew up in. High got tired of the maintenance on the original home. During one of our tours overseas, he had the old Victorian torn down and this modern home built in its place. It was the major argument of our married life. I could not believe the desecration, and I left him over it."

"Oh my."

"But not for long. He was not a man you abandoned if you wanted an interesting life. When I saw the masterpiece he had built in place of a decrepit monstrosity in 1951, I knew he was correct and I came home. We raised the children here, and it was much more convenient."

Plate glass windows made up most of the walls facing the water. "It doesn't look like a house from the 1950s," Amy said.

"We've modernized it twice since it was built. On the last remodel, Susan insisted we add the Internet and cable television." Mrs. Martin waved her bejeweled hand. "I prefer the books and the view. The modern world has too much noise in it, except for the marvelous organ at church. Darlin Poppins plays very well, doesn't she?"

"I enjoyed what I heard last Sunday. 'Great Is Thy Faithfulness' is one of my favorite hymns."

"God's faithfulness has been the key to my life, even when I was frightened for what would become of High or the children. See you in the morning."

"I'll leave my door open if you need anything in the night," Amy said.

"Thank you, my dear. I will not." Mrs. Martin went into the house.

Amy pulled her phone out of her pocket. No response from Josh since she had left her message. She bit her lip. Had Darlin given her the correct phone number? Or was he still angry with her?

She should have guessed Josh was a Navy SEAL, but with everything else so new, it hadn't occurred to her that he might not be the corpsman he claimed to be. Indignation burst in her chest. Had he told the truth about anything? Did the people at church know his true identity?

What about the pact they'd made? He'd pray for her and her fears, and she'd pray for him—about what? His words? Safety? She swallowed. She hadn't done him any favors with the bad tire on her car. He had warned her, he had gone through with her orders against his better judgment, and then his skill had saved their lives.

Amy looked at her phone again. He knew how to find her any day at six o'clock, but how could she ever find him? The clock in the hall chimed ten, reminding her of the library clock that ticked through her interview at the church.

Church. She'd find him there on Friday night, she thought. She'd see him in a safe place where he couldn't avoid her thanks.

Unless he didn't show up.

Chapter 17

SEAL stands for Sea, Air, and Land, but if in doubt on a mission, a SEAL headed toward the water. Josh liked the concept better in warm waters rather than in Southern California's Pacific Ocean. San Clemente Island, located about seventy-five miles northwest of San Diego was surrounded by cold water.

The sixteen-member platoon—two officers, one chief, and thirteen enlisted men—applied camouflage paint to their faces and swam onto San Clemente around four o'clock Friday morning. They cached their gear on the north end of the island, not far from the life-size model of a standard US embassy.

Their job was to take the "embassy" from the team currently defending it. As Josh had been at Balboa during the planning stages, he'd be mostly following orders and always prepared to help in a medical situation.

SEAL teams trained with live ammunition.

"Chief wants you to have a one-on-one with Flip as soon as you get a chance," Pete reported at oh-dark-thirty their second morning on the island.

"What's the problem?"

"You know Chief, he won't really say, but I think he's suspicious Flip lost his edge in the Gulf. He could be dangerous to the team."

Josh laced up his boots. "Why don't you talk to him? You're as qualified as I am."

"The team hasn't seen me kneeling down beside my sleeping bag to pray at night. They trust you more."

"My mother made me promise to kneel. You've seen how seriously the team takes it. Not."

"They know you pray and in this man's outfit, you're one of a kind," Pete said. "Flip's having trouble. He's afraid of getting hurt."

"No lie. It's dangerous out there, especially in the dark," Josh said.

"But Flip's been struggling. He's happier in a straight swim and demo than a land assault."

Josh couldn't catch Chief alone to confirm Pete's words, but often found himself paired with Flip. He tried to talk to Flip about personal issues apart from the mission. The man deflected his questions.

Long after midnight the sixth night, while they waited in an ambush situation, Josh tried again. His buddy shivered as he stared into the night. "You okay?" Josh asked.

"Do I have a choice? I'm obeying orders," Flip muttered.

"It can help to talk about what you fear. Knowledge is power."

Flip pushed up his night vision goggles and stared at Josh. "You got the quote wrong. G.I. Joe always said, 'knowing is half the battle.' "

"What are you talking about?" Josh asked.

"I forgot. You grew up without television in the boondocks."

"Boonville."

"Wherever. The only thing I fear," Flip said, "is letting

down the team and my family. I've got to keep my job for my family."

"Right." Josh knew Flip had struggled to get his mother, sister, and two nieces accepted as his military dependents. Once so designated, they'd moved into navy housing and now received medical benefits. One of the little girls had a health issue.

Flip held up his hand for silence.

While Josh remained on alert for the "enemy," he thought about Amy's fears and how she resisted the opportunity to reason her way out of them. The incident on the bridge would only make her worse, Josh realized. Should he try talking again to a frustrating woman who didn't want to change? But she sure was pretty, and something drew him to her in spite of common sense.

He'd pray for her. That's what he always did when she crossed his mind. It meant he'd discussed her quite a bit with God while training on the island.

Flip motioned and they scurried across the path. A pile of boulders farther up presented a better opportunity for shelter and surprise.

They had to crawl into a hole and through a thirty-inch-wide culvert to come out in a small opening under the rocks. Flip went first. When the soles of his boots disappeared, Josh groveled after him.

Was it the dust Flip kicked up that made Josh's throat spasm? Josh buried his nose in his camouflage jacket to stifle a sneeze and gulp more air.

His lungs felt constricted. Sweat prickled his brow under the helmet and goggles. What was this? All Josh could think of was the need to get out of the hole, the sooner the better.

"Use your brain, Josh," he whispered. "You just have to crawl another ten feet and you can stick out your nose next to Flip. There's nothing to be afraid of. Fresh air is just ahead."

He willed his body forward up a slight rise and could feel

the cool fresh air before he saw Flip lying in the opening.
Josh's heart raced, and he wondered if he was having a panic
attack. As he nestled beside Flip, he took deep breaths, full
and clear. Flip stabbed a look at him and then jerked his head:
a movement in the bushes.

Josh hid his mouth against his sleeve again. His breathing
sounded so loud, he was sure to give them away. He didn't
know how he'd be able to spring out of their hiding place to
seize the men. He needed to use his brain, not his emotions,
to get this job done.

A thin island fox jogged down the trail, glanced behind
him at something they could not see, and scampered into the
brush. A large figure loomed.

Flip burrowed close to the ground, and Josh heard him
gasp. They both put their heads down. A bright flash lit up
the area before them and they heard a shout. "Halt!" The
figure stopped, put up his hands, and the exercise was over.

"Close call, wasn't it?" Josh said. He grinned at his teammate.

Flip was weeping. With relief?

Josh scrambled out from under the boulders so the man
could be alone. But he understood.

Eight days later, they "hot roped" onto the North Island
Naval Base runway. Compared to the time he'd spent hiding
in the dirt and under rocks, sliding down a rope out of a he-
licopter was a literal breeze. The whole team, however, paid
attention to Flip's trip down. He managed fine that day, but
then, he wasn't boxed into a tunnel either.

Picking up his gear, Josh headed for the waiting navy bus.
He was glad to be back on a Friday afternoon and hopeful to
make it to the Bible study potluck. He'd enjoy seeing a pretty
face again after two weeks camping with his filthy platoon.

"I call the shower first," Pete said as they climbed on the
bus.

"You picking up your car?" Josh asked.

Pete groaned. "Tell me I left it here."

"Sorry. It's at NAB, remember? I'm going to have the bus drop me off on the corner near the house. You can have the shower when you get home." He laughed. "I've got to make brownies for the Bible study potluck tonight."

Pete snickered. "Don't go too domestic on me."

Josh saw Amy chatting with Carlos as soon as he entered the church's multipurpose room four hours later. Her hands moved as she talked, and she smiled with a freedom he hadn't seen before. In the long nights on San Clemente Island, he had not forgotten her smooth blond hair and cute nose. He grinned and walked right over. "Not having to worry about the bridge looks good on you."

Carlos laughed.

Amy put her hands on her hips. "Thank you for bringing it up. I'd almost forgotten about it."

"I didn't mean to bother you," he said.

"I know. Where have you been? Did you get my message?"

He set the brownies on the table. "Yes. I was happy to help."

"You saved my life. That's a big deal. You'll be happy to know I've got two new tires."

"Great. Bummer you don't have any place to go."

"No, it's not. I've been walking everywhere. I'm saving money on gas, wear and tear, and best of all, not worrying about getting to work. My life is so much better. Thanks."

"You got it." He liked watching Amy's eyes sparkle. It was good to see her happy.

He sat at the table with her, Lindsey, Carlos, and two female sailors stationed at NAB. He nudged Lindsey halfway through the meal. "You miss your roommate?"

She blushed and looked down at her plate. "Yes, but it's great to see her relaxed and happy again. It has to be making her a better therapist, not being so uptight. It also gives me an excuse to come over here and see all of you."

Lindsey had dimples. He liked them.

"Have you been training at the hospital all this time?" Amy asked. "Carlos thought you might have left Coronado."

Josh glanced at Carlos, who raised his eyebrows as if interested in a polite question. He shrugged. "We left the area on short notice. I never take my phone with me. Is it time for the study to begin?"

Carlos took the cue and they cleared the table.

The study wound down at eight forty-five, and folks made plans to see a movie at the vintage Coronado movie house on Orange Avenue. Josh yawned several times but not before noticing Amy and Lindsey flashing looks back and forth.

"Something up?" he asked.

"I have to go home," Amy said. "Part of my agreement is to be in by nine thirty in case Mrs. Martin needs me. I'm trying to convince Lindsey she can go to the movies without me."

"A fine friend I would be," Lindsey muttered, "abandoning Amy on a Friday night to take care of an old lady."

"I don't mind," Amy said. "It's a small price to pay to live here, and I like her."

Lindsey sighed.

"Go ahead, Lindsey," Josh said. "I'll walk Amy home. I've been up since four, and I'm ready to go to bed."

"I don't need you to walk me home," Amy sputtered. "Coronado is perfectly safe."

"You're right, but I live two blocks away from you so we might as well walk together." He stood up. "See you next week."

"Good night, Amy," Lindsey drawled.

"We're just going the same way," she said.

Lindsey winked. "I know."

As they ambled down the street, Josh had an idea. "Let's stop at Bottega Italiana."

"What is it?"

"Gelato shop. I'm partial to passion fruit," Josh said.

"I really need to get home."

"We can eat as we walk. Besides, passion fruit reminds me of you."

Amy followed him in the door. "What do you mean?"

He grinned. "Sweet and sour at the same time with a twist of passion. It's an intriguing combination. Just when you're savoring the sweet, it becomes feisty with a kick." He ordered two cones.

"That's how you see me?" She tilted her head.

"Don't you make people hurt for a living?"

"I ease their aches and tight muscles with massage," Amy said.

"And they all dance out of the spa, feeling good and bad at the same time, right?"

"You may be right." Amy took the cone from him as they exited and licked the yellow gelato. She opened her eyes wide. "Smooth sweetness with a tang of tart. This is delicious."

Josh clicked his cone against hers. "Finally, we agree on something. I'm glad. I've been praying for you."

"My problems are all over. I've conquered the bridge," Amy said. "And you've been so polite tonight. My prayers for you must be working."

Josh shook his head as they walked down the street. "Your phobia hasn't been conquered, Amy. You've just pushed it underground. We've got plenty of work left to do." He turned around when he realized she was not beside him. "Amy?"

She smashed the gelato cone into his nose and ran away.

Why did he keep trying to fix her? What business was it to him if she was afraid of the bridge? Why couldn't he leave her alone about it? Here she hadn't seen him in over two weeks and he wanted to talk about the bridge. What was wrong with this guy?

Amy dodged through the tourists sauntering on Orange Avenue and crossed the street past Panera Bread toward the residential area a block away. Her backpack banged against her as she sped in the direction of Mrs. Martin's house, and she felt breathless. The gelato taste—passion fruit—lingered on her tongue, and she regretted not finishing it. Why did he always make her so mad?

When she got to E Street she paused to catch her breath. Sticking that cone in his face should have caught him off guard, just like he'd done to her on the bus that first night. She took a deep breath and glanced over her shoulder to make sure she'd lost him.

"You said it was delicious. I assumed you liked it." Josh stood right behind her licking first one cone, then the other. "But if you don't want it back, thanks. This really is my favorite. I've only found it here and in Rome."

She snatched the cone from his right hand. "Rome, Italy?"

Josh held out the cone in his left hand. "This one was yours. Sorry for the nose print."

She swapped them and examined the gelato. "You've licked it smooth. When were you in Rome?"

He shrugged. "After a mission. I probably should finish the cone for you. No telling what germs I've picked up in my travels."

This was too intimate, licking the same gelato. Amy handed it back to him. "Go ahead. I shouldn't have smashed you with it. But you made me so mad."

"The problem is my mouth, like it said in the Bible study, out of the mouth comes both good and evil. I need to keep my tongue bridled. Have you been praying for me? I thought we made a pact."

The heavy scent of star jasmine filled the air, and lights went on in the house on the corner. Amy glanced at the clock near the Coronado visitor's center. "Do you know where we are? I need to hurry."

With a crunch, he demolished the top half of the first cone. Josh pointed up E Street with the second. "Let's take it all the way to First Street, hang a left, and you should be there in fifteen minutes. Right on time if we pick up the pace."

"I apologize again. I haven't prayed for your words," Amy said. "I've been praying for your safety. I couldn't remember what I said I'd pray for."

"Safety is always good in my line of work. Thanks."

"I'll do better, especially since you've been praying for me. Thank you."

Another crunch and he finished the cone. "I've been doing more than praying. I researched the subject in the medical library at Balboa hospital. Do you remember when your phobia began?"

She walked faster. They were at Sandpiper School, which meant she had a distance yet to go. "I really need to get home."

"Amy. Do you remember the first time you were afraid on a bridge?"

She didn't want to remember. But she knew. Oh, did she know.

When they got to the corner and had to wait for traffic to clear, Amy spoke slowly. "I haven't known you very long. I haven't seen you in a couple weeks. How can I trust you?"

She caught her breath when she looked up at him. Those blue eyes were focused on her, deep on her, even as he licked the second cone. It felt as if he could see into her very soul, a searing look that made her tremble. Remembering the strength of his chest and arms awakened a longing she didn't recognize. Strength? Security? She wanted to melt against him. But how could she trust him with the very worst memory of all?

Josh bit off the top of the second cone.

Amy saw the traffic had cleared and started across the intersection.

"Listen, Amy. I'm a corpsman, a medical guy. I'm also a Christian brother. I can see you're in pain, and I'd like to help you. Unfortunately, I'm not always going to be around to drive you across the bridge or trick you into riding the bus. Let me do a good turn by you and help you get over this. I won't laugh at you, and I'll bridle my tongue."

She walked faster. "What's in it for you?"

"The satisfaction of helping someone. We get tired of beating up the bad guys all the time. Sometimes we need to help the good women, so we'll feel good about ourselves."

As she continued down the street, past the narrow lots filled with houses of all sorts of styles—adobe, wood sided, mansion, hovel—Amy considered his words. He sounded genuine enough. He had proved his value in the car. If he was a SEAL, he wouldn't be around a lot anyway and she'd be going back across the bay to school at the end of the summer.

Amy peeked at him out of the corner of her eye. He was awfully good looking and way overconfident. But he had boyish humor about him that attracted her and infuriated her every time. She needed fun in her life.

Fun? He was proposing torture.

At Third Street, she looked east and saw the dotted golden lights of the black bridge arching up over the water a half mile away. The white lights marked cars headed down the bridge toward Coronado. Maybe she could try to avoid remembering the childhood incident on the bridge for the rest of her life. But she shouldn't. Wasn't it time to put bitterness and despair to rest?

He was so tempting, in too many ways.

She stumbled at the corner and Josh caught her arm. The same spark she'd felt the first time he touched her spilled through her with warmth again. She stared at him. What was this?

"Let me carry your backpack for you and feel like a real man. I can see you're thinking," Josh said.

"Okay." She slipped it off and handed it to him. "I hope it's not too heavy."

Josh laughed. "Not a chance."

They continued in silence to First Street, where they turned left, as he had said. When they reached the Martin gate, Amy faced him. "Okay. I'll take you up on your offer. When do we start?"

Josh yawned again. "Tomorrow's Saturday and I have it off. What time is your lunch break? I'll meet you on the beach in front of the spa. I'll even bring food."

"Brownies?"

He handed her the pack, leaned on the gate, and tapped her nose. "Maybe. What time?"

"One."

"I'll see you then." Josh saluted, jaywalked across the street, and was gone in a flash.

Amy leaned her head against the gate. What had she done?

Chapter 18

Ninety percent. Josh wrote the number on the wet sand with his finger, stood up, and faced the sea. Ninety percent of Navy SEAL marriages ended in divorce.

His job made life too complicated to involve a woman. He had no control over where he was sent, what he would do, or when he would go. The why was a given—he had sworn to do so, though people in a much higher pay grade made the decisions for him.

Tarzan's wife hated the navy, and her bitterness often spilled over to him, affecting the morale of the team. Their little boy, Tyler, suffered the most.

Flip had a widowed mother, a divorced sister, and two nieces who depended on him. Josh had just observed Flip's hesitancy during their most recent assignment. The man must be reevaluating his job in light of those females. Who could blame him?

The joke used to be "If the navy wanted you to have a wife and a family, they would have issued you one in your sea bag." For good reason.

Two attractive women in tiny bikinis sashayed past him

near the water. One pushed up her sunglasses and purred, "SEAL?" He looked out to sea again. It was easier that way.

Up until now, Josh had easily avoided romantic entanglements. The operational tempo made it hard even to meet women he might be interested in. But an attractive woman with big brown eyes had spun him around.

What was he going to do about Amy? He felt the lure of her personality and feisty spirit. He needed to be careful. He could get caught and this life was too hard. Maybe he needed to disappear again or ignore her. Josh looked at his hand. Then why was he carrying a Panera bag with lunch for two?

"I'm here!"

He turned at the sound of Amy's voice and checked his watch. Right on time. He had noted her determination to be responsible. He liked it. Too much.

Josh watched Amy release her shoulder-length hair from a hair device. It billowed around her rosy face in the breeze. She wore a pink tank top and white slacks. She seemed to be chewing her lower lip.

"What's up?" he asked when he reached her.

"The sand is a problem. I can't go back to work with sand on my shoes or on my clothes. Let's sit on this bench. Thanks for bringing lunch."

"No problem. I brought my favorite sandwiches."

"How fun. I wonder if I can guess what you planned for me. Chicken?"

Josh shook his head. "That's not what springs to mind when I think of you."

"No?" She nestled onto the white slat bench. "But you think of me?"

"I'm trying to keep America safe for people like you." He sat beside her and opened the bag. "Tuna salad or Italian combo?"

"I'm starving. I'll take Italian combo. Thanks again. I only have an hour, so I appreciate your punctuality."

"No problem." He'd chosen the Italian combo for himself, but he'd be gracious. He twisted the top off a bottle of water and handed it to her with the sandwich. Josh needed to keep his wits about him with this girl.

Amy took a swig of water and considered him long enough for him to twice breathe in a light honeyed scent. "Do you ever answer a question straight?"

"What do you mean?"

"See? Can't you just say yes or no? Let's practice." She took a bite of her sandwich and swallowed. "I could ask you, are you married?"

Josh could see his marks in the sand, just about the water line. A little boy ran by with a bucket and dunked it in the rippling water. The numbers would disappear soon. "Marriage is a wonderful thing."

"How about yes or no?"

Josh grinned. "I've never been married. How about you?"

"No. See how easy this is?"

"Maybe."

"Why didn't you tell me you were a SEAL?"

He took a bite of his sandwich and watched five sandpipers high-step along the sand washed smooth by the receding wave. When the water rolled in again, they scampered to the dry sand on their toothpick legs. "I'm a corpsman. Special Warfare Operations is my designator. We don't discuss our jobs with everyone we meet. Does it make a difference?"

"I don't know."

They ate in silence.

Amy cleared her throat. "Pete did talk about blowing things up the first time I met you."

Josh nodded. Pete always tried to impress women, and it irritated Josh. "That's one reason I seldom go to bars, other than the fact I don't drink alcohol. Drunks learn you're a SEAL and they want to start fights. It's stupid and pointless.

Besides, everything we do is secret, and mentioning our team just provokes questions."

"So if I ask where you were the last two weeks, you'll say you can tell me, but then you'll have to kill me?"

Josh smiled. "It would be so easy to kill you, too."

Amy leaned back. "What?"

He fingered the silver cross necklace around her neck and in so doing grazed her soft skin. Josh felt his heart rate zoom.

Years of practice helped control his breathing, and he spoke slowly in a soothing, almost seductive voice. "This is so tempting." He ran his finger under the chain to the back of her neck, modulating his breaths to bank the excitement.

Amy's deep brown eyes stared at him. She swallowed several times and licked her lips. "What do you mean?"

"All it would take is one swift jerk."

"Stop!"

He dropped his hand and grinned. "So tempting. You would be so simple to take out."

"I beg your pardon?"

"You started it. Of course I wouldn't kill you. There'd be far less legal entanglements if I just married you to shut you up."

Josh coughed. What did he just say?

"Ha. There's no way I'd ever marry you." She gestured widely with her sandwich. "I'd like to have a reasonable conversation with a husband instead of all the games you play. You never really answer questions, it's always verbal ping-pong."

His heart thumped harder. "So you admit you've thought about marrying me?"

He'd caught her. Her eyes widened, her mouth opened and shut, and she shivered out her answer. "Uh, no. I'd never consider it."

Josh laughed and watched a seagull coast along the waterline. A zodiac zoomed along the horizon, five men in black balaclavas riding the waves, and he sobered. "Good. You should stay away from guys like me. Our life is too difficult."

"In what way?"

"Operational tempos, can't talk about our work, forced camaraderie with the teams. There's not a lot of down time, and most SEALs haven't much practice with intimacy."

"I don't understand why it's so hard."

Josh sighed. "Special forces operators have a bad reputation for good reason. Someone's got to do the dirty work so you and your colleagues and my parents and everyone in America can have the freedom to live the life God called them to. All I am is a commando defending your liberties."

"Forever?"

"I don't know. I could get injured or maybe walk away when my enlistment ends in two years. Maybe God will change my situation. This is what I am today."

Amy put her sandwich wrapper in the bag and finished off her water. "I'm sorry, Josh, but thank you."

His phone vibrated in his pocket and Josh startled when he saw the number. "Excuse me, I need to take this. Corpsmen are like doctors, always on call for the team."

He walked toward the water as Chief's agitated voice came on the line. "We're at NAB headed for Balboa, Doc. We need you. Flip's in trouble."

"What happened?"

"He stopped breathing. We don't know why."

Amy didn't know what to think when Josh ran past her. "Later," he shouted and was gone.

So much for their date. If it was a date.

She gathered up the trash, dumped it in a nearby bin, and pulled out her own phone. Amy had twenty minutes left before she needed to return to work. She'd stroll along the promenade on the beach side of the hotel.

Vacationers with towels, toys, and children smelling

of sunscreen crossed her path on their way to the beach. The breeze blew her hair into her eyes. As Amy stopped to gather it back into a scrunchie, she heard her name. A guest at the Sun Deck Bar & Grill on the terrace above waved and shouted. Ethan.

"Don't go anywhere. I'm coming down," he called.

Why was he here? Amy's stomach turned over. He'd been an irritating pest at school, but this was a different scenario altogether. She frowned.

Always be polite to the guests, Amy knew the hotel drill. But did this apply to a guy from her psych class who had been chasing her all year long and never seemed to take no for an answer?

Amy turned her face away from the hotel and made a face. She hated pushy guys like Ethan. After avoiding him last semester, what would she say to him this time?

"Come join me for lunch," Ethan said. He stood nearly a foot taller than Amy, a skeletal white-blond guy with a red face and fast moving hands. "Where have you been? I've gone by your apartment a bunch of times and your roommate always says you're working."

She had to shield her eyes from the sun to look up at him. "I'm usually working. I'm on my break now and need to go back to work. See you another time."

"Where do you work? Here on the island? Hey, do you work at the Del's spa?"

"No time to talk. I've got to go. See you!"

She fled.

"You owe me a dinner. I'll meet you at the spa after work," he shouted.

Amy shuddered. She couldn't deal with him.

The first client after lunch was an enormous woman, Camilla, who probably weighed three hundred pounds. Obviously nervous, she apologized for her size as soon as Amy brought her into the massage therapy room.

Amy grabbed her hands. "I don't care how big you are, Camilla. Your body size has nothing to do with your worth as a person. All I care about is making you feel better after you've been here. I'm here to serve you for the next hour. Tell me what you need."

A tear dripped from Camilla's right eye. "I don't deserve this."

"A massage has nothing to do with deserving or not deserving, it's about making your muscles feel better and relaxing you. Do you have any injuries? Let's start. I'll knock on the door in a minute. Tell me when you're ready."

Amy closed the door and in the dim light of the hallway, leaned her head against it. "Too many emotions, Lord. Please help me focus on Camilla's needs. And whatever Josh's issue is, let him deal with it properly and safely. Oh, and help him keep his mouth shut when he needs to. Use my hands to Your glory. Amen."

She knocked on the door and entered at Camilla's muffled yes.

Camilla had requested the Spa at the Del's signature shell massage. Amy checked the heated tiger clamshells' temperature and then ran her hand along Camilla's body draped under the heated sheet and towel. "Have you had a massage before?"

"Not since I picked up all this weight. I had a massage once in China, and the woman told me I had shoulders of stone. They feel tight, so if you can concentrate there, I'd appreciate it."

"Women tend to carry tension in their shoulders and upper back," Amy explained. "For women and particularly computer users, the shoulders and the neck need the most work."

"You describe me perfectly." Camilla moaned. "It's been so long since my muscles have felt so relaxed."

Amy turned on Smetana's "The Moldau" on her CD player and turned the volume to low. She folded back the sheet, splashed warmed citrus oil on her hands, and pushed against the muscles in Camilla's legs with long strokes. Once she felt them loosen, she applied a heated smooth clamshell and pushed it along the skin, much like in a stone massage.

Closing her eyes to better "see" with her fingertips, Amy worked her way through the fat layers to muscle. She thought about Josh's suggestion that they get to the root of her fear—peel back the folds of her past and find what made the bridge so terrifying.

Amy would never forget the terrible argument her parents had while driving home late one foggy night over the Vincent Thomas Bridge. The shouting had gone on and on, and then her father stopped the car at the top of the suspension bridge.

"That's a sore place," Camilla said. "Can you work all through there around my angel wing? Push harder."

Amy shoved her memories aside, back under the layers of time, and applied herself to her job. Some things need to be left alone.

She could feel the knots near Camilla's right scapula. She prodded in a rounded movement at the tight muscle. This is where Camilla's extra weight made for difficulties. Amy switched to her right elbow and leaned the flat side into Camilla's back.

Camilla yawned. "I feel gloriously relaxed. I don't want to move."

"Then I've done my job well," Amy said.

"Oh, yes."

After Amy led Camilla to the hot tub, she returned to strip down the room and prepare for the next client. She lit a fresh lavender candle and cleaned the shells. Jackie entered. "There's a guy out here asking for you. He wants to know when you get off work."

Amy checked the temperature on the heated pad before she tossed a clean white sheet over the mattress. "A tall blond guy named Ethan?"

"He didn't say his name. When Kathy wouldn't give him

any information, he told her he wanted a massage and requested you. She said it wasn't allowed and you were all booked up until closing anyway."

Amy tucked in the top sheet and the cotton blanket. "Do I have clients all the way until six?"

"No. But she was trying to get rid of him. Who is he? I like Josh better."

"He's a guy from my psych class last fall. I let him borrow my notes each week because...well, it doesn't matter since he lied to me, but he's been inviting me out to dinner ever since to pay me back he says. I'd hoped he'd forget about me, but here he is."

She frowned. She didn't have time to waste on a guy who wouldn't take no for an answer. Amy put the used sheets in a bamboo basket under the countertop, sprayed rose scent into the air, and straightened her tunic. She needed to meet her next client.

Jackie walked with her to the front of the spa. "I'll tell him to go away. You can sneak out the back entrance when you're done."

Fear licked at Amy. Josh had said she needed to face her fears. She had two minutes before her next appointment. Amy marched to the spa front desk. She'd stare down this menace and be done with him.

Chapter 19

Josh heard the ambulance siren as he ran to Orange Avenue and crossed the street. He'd told Chief he'd be on the corner, and after the ambulance flashed by, Chief's red jeep slowed. Josh jumped into the back beside Pete, who was shivering and wet.

"What happened?"

Silence.

The veins bulged out of Chief's neck as they waited for the light to change. He tapped his fingers on the steering wheel and swore. They didn't have a siren, they had to obey the traffic laws, and it was killing Chief. He was through the intersection as soon as the light turned green and took the Fourth Street corner on two wheels. Chief swerved in and out of traffic and zoomed to eighty miles per hour going up the bridge.

It all happened so fast, the nerves were so palpable in the car, the sky so open on top of the bridge, Josh had to push back panic. "Why don't you slow down, Chief? If we get stopped by the police it will only take us longer to get to the hospital."

Chief growled and took his lead foot off the gas pedal.

They swooped through the curve toward town, and Josh was surprised to see bits of black tire still on the roadway.

"You'd told him he needed to face his fears," Pete finally said. "He wanted to push himself to prove he still has what it takes. Flip jumped in the pool with the BUD/S guys, swam through a tube and was tying ropes, like he's done a hundred times before. But this time…I don't know."

Josh frowned. "He was there because I told him to face his fears?"

"Didn't you?"

"Vaguely. I tried to joke with him, too. What were you doing at the pool?"

"Swimming laps. Chief came down to supervise Flip. We got him out of the pool fast…" Pete's voice trailed off. "I don't know what happened." He rubbed his eyes.

"What did he say to you, Doc? You must have got information out of him on San Clemente. I put you two together so you could sort him out." Chief's jaw moved up and down, and he took the turn off to I-5 in a hurry.

"He was worried about his family and not measuring up." Josh paused then added, "Maybe claustrophobia."

"That'll get you disqualified," Pete said.

Josh knew.

"You can't stiff your teammates like that. He needed to let us know," Pete said.

Chief, who should have been watching the freeway, glared at Josh in the rearview mirror. "Why didn't you tell me, Cubby?"

Cubby. He'd just been verbally demoted. "I'd planned to do some research to help him. I was going to start Monday morning. I knew he had trouble in the Gulf; but I figured we could talk it through."

"The command still needed to know. We can't risk other lives on a guy who may be a coward." Chief glanced over his shoulder and flipped on his blinker.

Josh tightened his jaw. "Flip's not a coward. He may have developed a phobia, but a phobia is curable. He'd need time with a psychologist, but it can be overcome."

Chief took the Balboa Park exit to the naval hospital. "Why were you looking things up?"

"He's got a girl who's afraid of the bridge. Doc is trying to help her," Pete said.

"On navy time?"

"On my own time," Josh said. "I was having lunch with her when you called. You should be glad; the Del was an easy place to pick me up."

"Let's hope you're not at the hospital all day, then." He swung into a parking spot, and they hurried to the emergency room.

They were there four hours. Once the medical professionals got all the water out of Flip's lungs and his breathing normalized, he was assigned a room. He'd start a battery of physical and psych tests the next day, but for the time being, he needed to sleep and his teammates were sent home.

Chief drove Pete and Josh back to Coronado— this time at a slower pace. Josh felt exhausted when they got home, but determined to attend church.

"Is it too late to get Darlin to play 'Great Is Thy Faithfulness'?" Pete asked. "I'm wiped out."

"Let's get dressed for church and find out. We need to thank God Flip's alive."

The stained-glass windows glowed from light inside the church when they drove up. As Josh trudged up the steps, his heart heavy, he heard the four-person praise group singing a song he recognized. The chorus mirrored events so closely, he stopped in the doorway: "And I will fear no evil for my God is with me. And if my God is with me whom then shall I fear?"

Pete bumped against him and grunted. "I still want 'Great Is Thy Faithfulness.' "

They walked down the right-side aisle to the first open

seats, and Josh slid in. Pete sat an arm's length away. Josh closed his eyes and leaned forward, his elbows on his knees and his face resting in his palms. He let the music soak in; he felt too exhausted to do anything more.

But his mind wouldn't rest. Was Flip in the hospital because of what Josh had said? He'd known the man was stressed and fearful, but had Josh pushed him beyond what he could take?

And was Josh as vulnerable as Flip?

"Am I a total idiot, God?" he whispered.

He heard Pete sniff. The guy was shell-shocked from working on Flip on the pool deck. He'd stayed steady through all the medical procedures at the hospital, never flinching as the medical personnel took blood and intubated Flip. Pete didn't like medical stuff, but he'd stayed beside his teammate. If Josh didn't feel so awful himself, he might try to reassure him.

But what reassurance did Josh have? *Did I say something that pushed Flip too far?* He'd asked himself the same question all afternoon long. His head ached and he wished he was five again and could climb into his mother's lap for comfort.

But he wasn't. Josh was a SEAL, and he knew bad things happened, even to good men.

He'd have to take it like a warrior. He couldn't risk his heart getting soft, or worse, giving in to fear himself.

He heard Pete shift, and a warm body settled beside him. He smelled the clean sweet scent Amy wore and felt a soft arm go around his back with warm comfort. Her voice whispered near his right shoulder. "It's okay. You're in a safe place."

Josh shut his eyes as tight as he could and shook. How long would he be in a safe place? Were there really any safe places for a man like him? Josh didn't know. He leaned on her gentle voice until the music came to an end three songs later.

Amy had her arms on both men. They were muscular, big men and she had to stretch. She rubbed Pete's back in slow, calming circles, while her left arm reached across Josh's shoulders. Josh's shaking unnerved her. "It's okay," she kept murmuring. "You're safe. You'll be okay."

She couldn't imagine what had devastated both men. Had someone died?

No one else seemed to notice. People stood around them, singing with their hands lifted high. In the dim light of the congregation, their far right side pew three rows from the back was even more shadowy. But with the music ending, the ushers would turn up the house lights and pass the offering plate.

Pete sniffed a few more times and sat up. He caught Amy's eyes and nodded. "Thanks."

She removed her right arm from Pete and leaned closer to Josh. "The lights are coming on. Will you be okay?"

He cleared his throat several times and nodded. Amy gathered her hands into her lap, rubbing right thumb over the left hand, and leaned back in the pew. Josh scratched his fingers through his black hair and straightened up. He fumbled in his pocket and pulled out his wallet. When the offering plate reached him, he dumped out all the bills and handed it to Amy.

"All your money?" she asked.

"Yes." His eyes were bloodshot.

Pete stared at the cross above the altar, so Amy handed the plate to the usher. Josh clutched her hand. He did not let go.

Amy tried to focus on Pastor Wayne when he entered the wooden pulpit, but the calloused hand gripping her fingers made it difficult as a sort of hot urgency flowed back and forth between them. At Pastor Wayne's opening remarks, though, Josh's tight clasp eased and their hands cooled to a friendly warm.

"I'm going to share concepts tonight from Billy Graham. My subject is fear," Pastor Wayne said.

"Fear is an emotion and has its place. It keeps us from making foolish choices and decisions. But it also can keep us from doing the very tasks God called us to perform."

Pastor Wayne told the story of the spies sent into Canaan to check out the land. Ten of them thought the giants made the place too terrifying to proceed. Two men, however, Joshua and Caleb, saw with different eyes—they recognized the obstacles, but were confident the God who sent them to scout Canaan would give them what they needed to conquer the land.

"Many of you can quote Bible verses about fear, like 'Cast your cares on the Lord and he will sustain you; he will never let the righteous be shaken,' from Psalm 55:22. I have a whole list of them. But like anything that upsets your soul, you need to get to the root cause of the problem. Billy Graham has several suggestions.

"Number one: Confront your fear and turn it over to Christ.

"Number two: Rely on God's promises—put your trust in them and not your circumstances.

"Number three: Pray diligently with faith. See me afterward if you need more scripture passages."

Pastor Wayne described how what-if thoughts can badger the most sane person into terror. Amy nodded.

She wasn't worried about falling off the bridge, though Amy knew it could have happened when the tire blew. Something else caused her terror, and the man beside her had volunteered to help her figure it out.

Pressed so close she could feel him breathing, Amy felt protective and full of awe.

Josh's expression had gone blank, but his eyes were riveted on Pastor Wayne. Pete now leaned in the corner of the pew with his arms crossed over his chest. His face, too, showed no emotion, but she could almost see his brain clicking. Fascinating. Both of them.

"Finally, pay attention to Philippians 4:6–7: "Do not be anxious about anything, but in every situation, by prayer and petition, with thanksgiving, present your requests to God. And the peace of God, which transcends all understanding, will guard your hearts and your minds in Christ Jesus."

Pastor Wayne smiled as he pronounced the benediction. "There is hope for your future and your present even in the midst of the most anxious difficulties. Put your trust and faith in the hands of the One who loves you, knows you, and understands your situation. Ask Him to show you what to do. He'll answer your prayers."

The praise team played only one song to end the night. In a holy hush without music, the congregation crooned, "Great Is Thy Faithfulness."

In the middle of the final verse, Josh dropped her hand, climbed out of the pew, and jerked his head toward the door. Pete joined him and they headed for the exit. Amy scurried to the back pew, grabbed her purse, and followed. She caught up to them as Pete opened the car doors.

"Wait," she called. "Where are you going?"

Josh glanced at the church. The worshippers would soon exit. "This isn't a good night for us to meet people. We need to go."

"Can I come with you? I'd like to know."

Josh hesitated. "Sure. Get in the car."

Pete started the engine before she got her seat belt fastened and they took off. "Where to?" he asked.

"We'll take her home."

"Are you going to tell me what happened?" Amy asked.

"No."

They stopped at the traffic light on the Orange Avenue corner and both men peered at McP's outdoor patio. "I don't see anybody," Pete said. "Chief will probably call a meeting tomorrow."

Josh pulled out his phone and scrolled through the messages.

"The city lights are beautiful at night," Amy said. "You're

welcome to sit on Mrs. Martin's patio and be quiet. I was going to make cookies. I won't bother you."

Could these men talk without speaking? What kind of shorthand went on between them? A curt nod from Josh to Pete.

"Thank you, Amy," Pete said as the light changed. "I need to do something else tonight, but I'll leave Josh with you."

"I'm not talking," Josh said.

"How refreshing," Amy said with a sad shake of her head.

Chapter 20

Was this a good idea? Josh stood on the doorstep beside Amy and didn't know. He wasn't ready to go home, but he didn't really want to talk to anyone. He knew Pete needed alone time to process the afternoon. So he was at Amy's house on a beautiful Saturday night, trying to be optimistic. Maybe Mrs. Martin would distract him, she often said witty things. Chocolate chip cookies warm out of the oven might make him feel better.

Church had helped, but nothing was sorted straight in his mind yet.

Amy kept glancing at him, but wasn't saying much. He tried to remember lunchtime and the heady excitement of seeing her. What were they supposed to talk about? How to deal with fear?

Josh had quite a negative track record on that subject at the moment.

Amy opened the door and ushered him in. He followed her through a stunner of a house—the living room alone was the size of his parent's cottage in Boonville—and out onto a patio facing the extraordinary lights of downtown San Diego. Josh whistled—it seemed appropriate—but stopped his lips when he caught Mrs. Martin's upraised right eyebrow.

"Good evening."

"I'm Joshua Murphy from church, ma'am. I've never been in a house with such a magnificent view."

She regarded him with unblinking eyes. "Oh, yes. I remember seeing you. You are here with Amy?"

"Yes, ma'am."

"What do you do for a living? I believe I've recommended the military to you in the past."

"I'm a navy corpsman, special forces."

"A corpsman saved my husband's life once. They tend to be brave and selfless, going into harm's way to provide medical care in the field. Have you ever saved anyone's life?"

What a question on a night when he felt guilty for nearly killing someone. Had he ever saved anyone's life?

"Yes." He stood straighter. "Twice in the last year."

"Really?" Amy gasped. "Who?"

Mrs. Martin's lips twisted and she watched him. He held her eyes and kept his mouth shut.

"Very good." She laughed. "He can't tell you, Amy. It probably was a secret operation."

"Operation?" Amy asked. "You performed an operation?"

"Stand down," Mrs. Martin ordered.

"When do I get my cookies?" Josh asked Amy.

"I'll get right on it." She hurried away.

"Have a seat," Mrs. Martin said. "I've held security clearances in my time. I'd like to hear about your escapades."

Josh took a rattan chair close to the woman. He watched the lights glimmer across the bay. He saw a ship pass and the ferry glide to the dock around the bend. The old woman's lips were moving, but he couldn't hear her words. "Are you praying?"

Mrs. Martin nodded. "I'm waiting to hear stories of how God has used you."

"I haven't been well used today."

"It doesn't have to be today. What can you talk about? I want to be encouraged."

Josh blew out his cheeks. Encouragement would be helpful. What could he tell her, a woman who probably had seen and heard everything? An old lady who daily watched a spectacular view of sea and sky and bright lights probably couldn't be surprised by much. What story could he share?

Josh sat back in the chair. "Let me tell you about my life before I joined the navy. I lived in a magical place of shaggy redwood trees beside the Navarro River. I worked part-time as an EMT, and I saved a lot of lives."

By the time Amy returned with cookies hot from the oven, Josh and Mrs. Martin had laughed over his rural childhood, shared reflections on tragic auto accidents, and connected on the virtues of crisp tangy apples. He felt much better. Maybe he wasn't as awful a loudmouth as he thought.

The cookies tasted delicious.

"I'll be heading to bed now. Thank you for entertaining me, Petty Officer Murphy."

Josh stood and held out his elbow. She took his arm and he led her back through the fancy living room to the hallway. "This is far enough," she said. "A woman needs her privacy." She shook her finger at him. "Behave yourself."

Josh presented his best salute.

"Stand down. I've enjoyed our visit."

Amy stood by the water's edge when he returned. "Thank you," he said when he joined her. "I needed that."

"What did you talk about?"

"I told her stories. She enjoyed them, and it helped me forget a miserable day."

Amy took his hand. "Whatever it is, I'm sorry."

He closed his eyes and, yet again, felt some sort of connection with Amy's strong, comforting hands. The healing profession so often was an art more than a science, even though

Josh preferred to stay in the logical realm. But something happened when she touched him, a hot lick of excitement and contentment, and he didn't want her to stop.

Still, what could he say? Josh went to straight facts. "As a corpsman I'm on call for the team and their families. I keep track of the men's health and carry a medical kit when we're working. Their health is my responsibility. Flip got hurt, but he's in the hospital now, and they'll take good care of him."

"You and Pete seemed so upset, I thought someone had died."

Josh looked at her beautiful, concerned face. "He nearly died. Possibly because of something I said."

She gasped.

"I told you. I'm dangerous. We should probably end this before it becomes more serious."

She looked down at their clasped hands and whispered, "I don't want to."

Josh leaned closer. "What?"

Amy tossed back her hair and looked at him with determination. "You told me I needed to face my fears. You're one of my fears, Josh Murphy. But you promised to help me get over the bridge fear and I trust you. I need you. Please?"

Warmth spread through Josh's body, starting from his heart. "I don't know what to say."

She laughed. "You're speechless?"

"Right now I'm going to be a man of action."

He lost both his pain and fear in that one sizzling kiss.

Amy relived the kiss all day on Sunday.

When her first client smelled like she hadn't bathed in days, Amy didn't flinch and remembered the kiss.

When her second client felt ticklish and couldn't lie flat, Amy smiled and remembered the kiss.

When Jackie asked her if she was feeling okay, Amy remembered the kiss and shook her head. "I'm better than okay. I'm perfect."

"Really? Kathy was concerned you didn't take her reminder to better treat the guests as seriously as you should have."

That got Amy's attention. "I was polite. I marched Ethan out of the spa and asked him to never come back again."

"She didn't realize he was a stalking boyfriend with no plans to actually pay for a massage until I told her, but she did say you should keep your personal life separate from your work life. I'm just passing along a warning. The guests are always right."

"Ethan's not my boyfriend. He was here for lunch, not staying in the hotel. But if it ever happens again, I'll be more professional."

Jackie touched her arm. "You look different. What's happened to you?"

"I'm empowered. I faced my fear with Ethan and sent him on his way. Overbearing guys like Ethan have scared me my whole life. Then I took on Josh." She grinned. "It was very good."

"Did you scare him away, too?" Jackie looked doubtful.

Amy collected a pile of clean sheets to take to her therapy room. "I hope not. I've joined forces with him, and he's going to help me."

When she got home at six thirty and entered the house, Amy heard Josh's voice in the kitchen. "Courage and valor are part of military life."

Amy stood in the shadows to watch the man who had kissed her so well. She tingled all over again. He looked so handsome, even with an apron tied around his taut middle. He waved a wooden spoon.

"True, but it's manageable." Mrs. Martin sat at the breakfast table with a glass of lemonade. "Remember what General Patton said: 'All men are frightened. The more intelligent they are, the more they are frightened. The courageous man is the man who forces himself, in spite of his fear, to carry on.' "

Josh stirred a pot on the stove smelling of onions, garlic, peppers, and tomatoes. Amy's stomach rumbled. "That may be more difficult than it sounds," he said.

"Nonsense. You use your mind and your soul together to confront terrifying situations. High was afraid to climb into the cockpit after being shot down the first time. He had nightmares about not being able to get out in a fire."

"Really?"

"He drove himself to conquer the fear so he could perform. The old house had a small closet under the stairs. He went in there, closed the door and stayed as long as he could bear it. Often he'd come out soaked in sweat."

"Was it claustrophobia?" Josh asked.

"Perhaps. I would time him to see how long he could stay in the closet. We practiced every day. Once High could last an hour, he went to the airfield and sat in airplanes. It was a frightening time. He was not a coward, but the mental agony he went through might have made his senior officers think he was."

Josh focused on the pot.

Mrs. Martin chuckled. "High didn't like George Patton, but he used another one of his quotations often: 'Courage is fear holding on a minute longer.' It helped him work through his uneasiness."

Josh noticed Amy. "What do you think? We could work in tiny steps to handle the fear?"

Amy set down her backpack. "I don't think the CHP would allow me to drive across the bridge a minute at a time."

He reached into his pocket and pulled out his smartphone. "Pete and I went over the bridge this morning and made a movie. Watch it and see how you react."

She took a chair beside Mrs. Martin, showed her the phone,

and touched the black arrow in the middle of the screen. "Look, they're driving down Fourth Street."

The elderly woman shook her head. "You made a little movie and put it on your telephone?"

"The telephone made the movie," Josh said. "I just pushed the button. How you doing, Amy?"

She watched the boring film of them driving down the street. She heard Josh point out the U-turn spot in case someone changed their mind. On the video, the bridge was a ribbon of gray bordered by blue sky, with a faint rumble of the road and slight shake of the picture. It didn't bother her at all.

"I've never noticed those suicide hotline signs before," Pete said on the video. "Do you remember Tarzan's story about the guy he saw jump off the bridge?"

"This is supposed to be a dull film showing how safe the bridge is," Josh replied on screen. "Ignore him, Amy."

She smiled. The little film went on for three minutes. A car driving down a street between two gray sets of barriers. She couldn't tell they had gone up in the air. Easy. Simple. Nothing to be afraid of.

Amy returned the phone to its owner. "No problem. Am I cured?"

Josh grinned. "Want to try it? You can drive."

"No, thanks." She mirrored his smile. "I need more practice."

"Good. You've got the idea. Watch it again while I cook the pasta. This process is called desensitization. We put you, safely, in the situation that triggers your anxiety a little at a time until it stops bothering you. If we work on it every day, getting closer and closer to our goal, one day you'll be able to drive over the bridge."

She set down the phone. "Are you going to be around every day to help me?"

He hesitated. "I can't make any promises. If I deploy for any length of time, I'll leave you the phone."

"Don't you need your phone?"

He shook his head as he stirred the angel hair pasta into boiling water. "We don't take phones on missions. The GPS feature would give away our location."

Amy went to the sink to wash her hands. "Then how do you call?"

"We don't call." Josh whisked a solution in a mug and poured it over the green salad.

"Never?"

"We occasionally visit Internet cafés and send e-mail; otherwise, once we're gone, we're gone. I told you SEAL duty was hard on families, but Josie had it much worse during the wars."

"Josie?" Amy asked.

Mrs. Martin didn't blink an eye. "Absolutely. In 1944 I only received twelve letters from High."

"You counted them?" Amy collected the dishes and brought them to the table.

"One a month. Hand Joshua the colander from under the sink."

"Where did you learn to cook?" Amy asked Josh.

"Boy Scouts. All my helpful skills come from the Scouts." He drained the pasta, put it in a shallow bowl, and poured on the sauce. "Time to eat."

Josh regaled them with stories from his childhood in the woods, outlined his thoughts on desensitizing Amy to the bridge, and asked his new pal Josie for stories about her husband. Amy, who was hungry after a full day of clients, ate silently, enjoying the banter between the two. Mrs. Martin, as sharp and lively as ever, was flirting with the man at her table. Amy tried not to let it bug her.

"I'm so glad Susan is on a business trip this week. She'd be boring you with mathematic equations or harping on the state of the economy."

"Might be interesting to hear what she has to say," Josh said. "If she's your daughter, she must be charming."

"She's her father's daughter: efficient and to the point."

"How about you, Amy? Are you your father's daughter?"

Amy froze with her fork halfway to her mouth. Where had his question come from? Heat rose in her face, and her heartbeat quickened. "No. I'm not like my father at all. Are you?"

Josh's eyes narrowed as if he was appraising her. "I hope so. He's a good man."

Mrs. Martin reached for her teak cane. "I will leave you two in here while I go outside to watch the light change. Thank you for dinner, Joshua, and please say good-bye before you leave."

Josh kissed her hand and helped her up. He walked her out, promising to bring her a cup of tea. Amy watched them with mixed emotions. Men never stayed. Women's hearts were always expendable. In her irritation, she had all the dishes loaded into the dishwasher by the time Josh returned.

"Now there's a great lady. Wise, too."

"Yes." Amy sharpened her voice. "Why are you a SEAL?"

His face went blank and his voice hollow. "Why do you ask?"

"I've been wondering about it ever since I figured out what you do. I don't understand how you can work such a vicious job." Her fingers trembled as she dumped the cutlery into the silverware container. "Do you like disappearing at the drop of a hat?"

When he didn't answer, she faced him.

"I have an honorable profession, done with the best of my integrity, with good men who love their country." His voice sounded stiff.

"Really? I thought you were protecting us from the bad guys."

"That is my job. To project you and everyone else in America from the bad guys."

Amy reached for the saucepot and filled it with hot soapy water. "Who are the bad guys? Someone you define as a bad guy. Now you'll march out Osama bin Laden and probably Hitler who's been dead for a hundred years."

"Hitler died sixty-six years ago."

"Whatever. The point is you and your teammates apparently prowl the world looking for excuses to blow up people. I wonder if you like it."

He shook his head. "I don't like it."

"Then why are you a SEAL? You told us last night you'd saved two lives. Have you ever killed anyone?"

Josh cleared his throat.

She stared. "Aren't you going to say anything?"

He shook his head.

Amy felt like cold seawater had been thrown over her and her stomach clenched. "Have you killed anyone?"

"You don't have a need to know. I can't say, even if I wanted to."

"You have?" She recoiled and suddenly felt as if something important had crumpled into nothing.

He looked at her with steely eyes that made her tremble in a not-so-good way. "I'll tell you," he said quietly.

Amy slumped. Was this good or bad? "I don't think I want to hear."

He grabbed her wrist and drew her hand to his lips, where he placed a gentle, warm kiss. "You need to hear this story."

Tears rose in her eyes. He led her back to the table where he motioned for her to sit down.

"I told you about growing up in the countryside, living in a state park, and roaming at will with my best friends. It was a terrific childhood. But those back hills are good places to hide for people who weren't interested in obeying laws. I call people who break the law on purpose bad guys."

"Okay," Amy whispered, never taking her eyes off his face.

"When we outgrew the state park and my best friend's

apple orchard, we started taking longer hikes. We'd pack lunches and hike for hours. Usually it was Sean and Amos and me. One time Amos's younger brother, Jedediah came. He was twelve. We were fourteen."

Amy nodded.

Josh broke eye contact and stared toward the glass windows where San Diego's lights shone. He described a warm September day when the brown grass covered the hillsides against a startling blue sky. They had hiked along the hilltops and were headed into a ravine only a couple of miles from downtown Boonville.

"We were ticked off Jedediah had followed us. He kept making stupid jokes and acting like a little kid, which I suppose he was. We decided he needed to learn his lesson. If he was going to hang out with us, he needed to grow up."

Josh swallowed. "Amos and Sean and I had been out late the night before, and we got tired. We'd run out of water, so we gave him our canteens and pointed down a thin trail in the grass. 'Go get us water.'

"He whined, but Jed was a good kid, homeschooled like the rest of us. We were Boy Scouts and knew about the buddy system—you never go anywhere without your buddy—but we were lazy. I told him he had to go by himself."

"What happened?" Amy barely breathed out the words.

"I don't know if we fell asleep or not, but suddenly I realized he'd been gone too long. Water shouldn't have been far away. I headed down the trail to find him. I heard him shout and then two shots." Josh sniffed and swallowed again.

"Amos and Sean heard them, too. We got on our bellies and slithered through the grass down the hill. Jed had stumbled onto a marijuana farm."

His words faltered, and he cleared his throat several times.

"Sean ran for help, but it would take him twenty minutes to get to a phone. The guys who shot Jed had guns. We knew they would shoot us, too. Amos and I watched Jed bleed on the ground until the good guys came."

"Was he dead?" Amy whispered.

"He died at the hospital. He'd lost too much blood. That's why I don't care about bad guys. They shot a twelve-year-old kid I sent down to the creek for water. There are a lot of bad guys out there, and I was responsible for them killing a good kid who just wanted to hike with some Boy Scouts."

She rubbed her hands together. "I'm sorry, Josh."

He shrugged. "It was a long time ago, but I'll never forget him."

She nodded in sympathy, but her hands shook. She should have known he carried ghosts in him. Didn't everyone?

Chapter 21

"Thanks for coming, Doc," Flip said when Josh walked into his hospital room Monday afternoon. "I appreciate you guys bailing me out of the pool."

"Pete and Chief saved you. I caught up at the ER." He took the chair beside the bed. "How're you feeling?"

"Fine. Have they let you see the psych eval?" Flip stared at his hands, clenched in front of him but shaking. "Can you spring me? I need to get back to the team."

"I've come to get you. We're going to stop on the way home for virtual reality therapy."

Flip blinked rapidly. "Why?"

"Look, Flip, what happened in the Gulf shook up a lot of us. It was tough getting caught in a cramped space. Claustrophobia can be dealt with, and the navy's got a group to help." Josh watched the reaction.

Negative.

"Don't go blank on me," Josh said. "This can be taken care of."

"That's not my problem."

"What is your problem?" Josh leaned back in the chair and stretched his legs.

"I ran out of air. I was fixated on the knot tying. I'm okay. I need to get out of this hospital."

Flip wasn't the most robust-looking guy in the best of situations—which was why people never suspected he was a SEAL—but his darting eyes and agitation concerned Josh. Something still bothered Flip.

As Josh knew only too well, SEALs are excellent actors. He handed Flip a bag. "Here's your clean uniform. I'll wait outside." He closed the door as he left.

"Well?" Chief asked when Josh joined him in the hall.

"Chart says lungs are clear. He's denying any problems, as you probably heard."

Chief nodded. "What'd you think about the virtual reality place?"

Josh scratched the back of his neck. "They're doing great stuff with posttraumatic stress disorder, and they said incidents like the one in the Gulf can trigger PTSD in bystanders. The therapist walked me through the routine for anxiety issues like claustrophobia, and they'll do a thorough intake at three o'clock if he's willing. They got his eval while I was there and think it can work. Your call."

Chief Rossi was a solid, strong man with a heart-shaped tattoo on his chest that read "Annie." He bragged he got a three-fer with his tattoo: his mother and wife were both named Anne, and he named his only daughter Analiese. He could be as hard as nails in a military setting, and Josh had seen him do things no one ever talked about.

But he loved his teammates and they trusted him, even when they didn't like him. Josh knew he would be fair and would take into account both Flip's needs and those of the navy.

"How'd you handle it?" Chief asked.

"Me?" Josh flinched.

"You said they put the goggles on you. You were caught in the same incident that started this. How'd it affect you?"

Josh's stomach churned. What did Chief suspect?

He cleared his throat. "It all made sense to me, and the goggles"—he held up his hands on either side of his head to demonstrate—"were bulky so it didn't feel natural. The pictures were of the quality you see in a video game, but realistic enough. They had a submarine missile tube simulation if we need it. Talking to Flip will give them a better idea of how the treatment will proceed. Ten weeks and he should be fine."

Chief frowned. "We need him to get better fast. Ten weeks is a long time to have him gone. Think you can get him moving faster?"

"Something's motivating him. Maybe."

"The navy's invested too much in his training, and I don't want to lose him. You take him over the next couple weeks to make sure."

"Me?"

"We can't afford to lose you either, Doc." Chief held his eyes a moment longer than necessary, and then turned when the door opened. "Good to see you, Flip. Let's go."

Josh heaved an enormous sigh of relief when he reached home at seven thirty. The day had been exhausting, what with battling traffic, learning about Flip's therapy requirements, touring the facility, meeting Chief for Flip's discharge, and then returning with the reluctant sailor to the therapy center. Flip was determined to conquer his fears, which was a great sign, but it would take time.

"Man chili on the stove," Pete said when Josh entered the apartment. "I put in plenty of meat. What's up with Flip?"

Josh stripped off his camouflage uniform jacket and hung it on a peg. Pete made a mean chili with lots of spices, and his mouth watered. "He failed the first test leaving the hospital, but there's hope."

"What test?" Pete muted the TV.

"Chief must have been reading up on the subject. He gave Flip the choice: elevator or stairs. Flip looked like a caged dog and said the stairs were best since he hadn't done PT in two days."

"Sounds reasonable to me."

Josh filled a bowl and stuck it in the microwave. "One of the first signs of claustrophobia is fear of an elevator."

"You have trouble with an elevator?"

"Me? Of course not."

"Just checking," Pete said.

Josh carried his hot bowl to the table, tossed on cheese, and paused at the chopped onion.

"I dare you," Pete said.

"It's not what you think."

Pete laughed. "Right. You going to see her tonight?"

Josh looked at his watch. "Only if I eat fast. Probably not." He stirred the chili and then sighed. "You know, it was bad in the Gulf."

"Yep."

"Did you think about that diver when you pulled Flip out of the water on Saturday?"

"Yep."

"The diver panicked with us all wedged into a tight tube with him. You could see it in his face," Josh said.

Pete turned off the television and stood up. "*You* saw something in his face. I was trying to find a way out before we died. If Flip hadn't figured out how to get us through that hole, we all might have bit the bullet."

"What's never made any sense is why the diver panicked. I've gone over it countless times. Flip and I talked about it on San Clemente Island. We never figured it out."

"You told Chief you didn't talk to Flip," Pete said.

"We didn't talk specifically about what bothered him, but we did talk about what happened in the Gulf." Josh tossed onions onto his chili and took a bite.

"There's nothing wrong with asking for help. Isn't that what you always tell us, Doc?" Pete finally said. "Take advantage of all those therapy meetings you're attending with Flip. Chief's sending you on purpose."

"I kind of thought I'd see you last night," Amy said when she opened Mrs. Martin's front door to Josh late Tuesday afternoon.

"You got my text?" Josh asked.

"Yes. I understood. How is Flip?"

Josh put up his hands. "Confidential. I can't say."

"Forget I asked."

"The therapy is interesting, and I'm getting insights for you. No other need to know." Josh followed her into the kitchen where she picked up a tray of fresh-cut vegetables and headed toward the patio.

Amy felt self-conscious about every movement with him behind her. The hem of her skirt swayed against her knees with the movement of her hips. The wisp of breeze tossed the short tendrils about her face into her eyes. She licked her lips and thought about the kiss.

No. She needed to stay focused. He had come to help her with the bridge after dinner. The fact she had spent a large portion of her two days off cooking was a coincidence. She wanted to pay him back adequately. She glanced over her shoulder.

He looked docile enough as he followed, except for the shadow of a grin dancing across his lips.

Don't look at his lips!

She met his eyes.

Amusement danced there, too, ocean-blue eyes gazing at her under black brows. "Do you need me to open the door for you?"

"Oh," Amy turned back toward the slider. The door was

open wide to the patio, where Mrs. Martin waited. "The door isn't closed," Amy said.

"I know, but I couldn't imagine why else you paused in front of it." Josh touched the tip of her nose. "You're not a very good actress, Amy. And yes, you look very nice in your dress."

Mrs. Martin tapped her cane on the flagstone patio and laughed. "This is your appetizer and then you go. Amy will put the casserole in the oven, and we'll eat when you get back. She made an apple pie."

Josh grabbed a handful of carrot sticks. "Pete will be jealous."

"Bring him with you one night," Mrs. Martin said. "I like having men in uniform around."

"Keep your eyes peeled and you'll see some Thursday night," Josh said.

She nodded. "It's Hell Week, isn't it?"

He tossed an olive into the air and caught it in his mouth.

"What are you doing?" Amy asked.

"I thought I was the free entertainment. I'm paying for my supper."

She glanced at Mrs. Martin.

"Thursday night is usually the around the world," Mrs. Martin said to Josh.

"Yes," he said. "Can I do an angel launch from here?"

Mrs. Martin bowed her head as if bestowing a regal favor. "It would be an honor to assist you. What time? I would like to supervise."

Josh shrugged. "One or two. I don't know. I thought I'd camp out until I heard them coming."

"Fine. I haven't sat a vigil in a long time. I'll pray for the men this week," she said.

"What are you talking about?" Amy asked.

"Hell Week. It doesn't concern you."

"If it concerns Mrs. Martin, why wouldn't it concern me?"

"With any good fortune, my dear, you may be a navy wife someday, and then you'll understand." Mrs. Martin looked at Josh.

He shook his head. "You know better than most how difficult the life is."

"True. But when she loves a good man, a woman can put up with a lot."

Amy put her hands on her hips and stamped her foot. "Now you've got Mrs. Martin talking in riddles. Stop it. I'm not a child."

Mrs. Martin smiled. "Go work on your bridge assignment before it gets too dark."

Amy shoved the casserole—browned pork chops and onions nestled on a bed of tiny potatoes, carrots, and peppers—into the oven. They had ninety minutes to complete the task she had little interest in pursuing at the moment.

She stomped out the front door past Josh, who closed it gently behind them, and smacked the button to open the gate. Turning left, she stormed down the sidewalk headed east toward the bridge.

"Ease up," Josh called. "We've got plenty of time. It's only a twenty-minute walk to Tidelands Park."

"I don't want to talk to you. You always imply I can't do enough, I'm not strong enough. There's always some sort of mystery going on I can't know anything about."

He shrugged. "That's the way it is. You got to face facts and there are some facts you can't know."

"Why can't I know them? You don't think I have what it would take to live a military life? I know what it's like to live without a man in the house. I've done well, thank you."

Josh gestured to the east. "We'll cross that bridge if we come to it."

Amy shook her head. "You're always making fun of me, but I'm strong. God has taken me through plenty of hard things."

"I'm sure He has. I'm impressed you took the job on this island with your fears. Let's work on the bridge, and we'll see what you're made of."

She whirled around and crossed her arms. "What if I tell you I don't want to? I don't like your tactics, and I'll live with it?"

He matched her stance. "I'll say, 'Okay. Go ahead.' I'll go home, and you won't see me again. Is that what you want?"

Actually, she wanted another kiss, but she knew she couldn't say so. She tapped her foot and watched him even as traffic picked up on the street and a small brown bird flitted past to rest in a flowering bird of paradise bush.

He was good at waiting. He looked like a statue in a brown polo shirt and black cargo shorts. His tanned legs were like stone and even his toes encased in black sandals didn't fidget.

Amy shut her eyes. What did she really want? Deep down, what was important here?

She gave a curt nod. "I want to beat the bridge."

"Good." Josh grabbed her arm, and she tingled again. "Let's go."

They walked down Third Street past apartment buildings, houses, and eventually Sharp Coronado Hospital, before arriving at the green ball fields of Tidelands Park. Games were in play, but Josh didn't watch, taking her past the children's play area and parking lot to the bay itself.

Above to the right, the bridge loomed, filled with evening traffic headed off the island. Josh pointed. "What do you see?"

"The bridge."

"How do you feel?"

"Fine. Are we done?"

He grinned. "Let's examine it a little more." They walked along the Silver Strand bikeway that ran down the east side of the island. Small sailboats bobbed in the blue bay on their left, and bike riders flashed by in a steady stream on their right. Overhead, Amy could hear the clatter of cars accelerating up the rise. Josh stopped every fifty yards to ask, "What are you feeling?"

"Nothing." Amy was pretty sure the physical bridge was not the source of her panic, but she didn't know how Josh could help her with the real issue. Still, she let him try.

"This is a pre-stressed concrete girder bridge," Josh explained, "not a suspension bridge like the Golden Gate. Did you notice the railing is only three feet high when we stood on the bridge after the tire blew?"

"It scared me to look over the side."

"The bridge isn't designed for pedestrians. You're not supposed to be out of your car up there. We can't walk over it, but we can take the path and get close. Let's try it."

They walked under the bridge, and Josh described how it was built. She shoved on a sturdy pillar. She shouted at the bridge, told the bridge she wasn't afraid of it, and then they went home.

"How was it?" Josh asked when they reached the gate to Mrs. Martin's house.

Amy took a deep breath. "I enjoyed being with you once we got past the first issue. You were kind, generous, thoughtful, and smart. I know all about the Coronado Bridge now. Thank you."

"But how do you feel?" Josh asked.

Amy's heart pounded. She could not look at his mouth, but his eyes were dangerous, too. Could she trust him?

"Amy?"

She swallowed. "I'm going to need more time."

Josh put his elbow on the gate and leaned in her direction.

Amy's eyes grew big. He was leaning in to her and so very close she could feel his breath on her face. Every sense went on yearning alert and she licked her lips.

He touched the tip of her nose again. "I'll give you all the time I've got."

Chapter 22

"That was bad," Josh said as they walked out the NAB gate headed toward home Thursday afternoon.

"Yep," Pete said.

"Did you know what happened when you were out there delivering candy last night?"

"No. High seas. It was dangerous, as you heard." Pete squinted in the direction of the beach. "Cold, too, but you expect it. With the fog rolling in now, it should be an interesting night for those guys."

"That's what BUD/S Hell Week is all about."

"Yep."

They continued in silence up Orange Avenue, pausing to chat briefly with several SEALs from other teams who were having a cold one in the McP's patio. When they finally got to the light on the corner, they found Pastor Wayne waiting for them.

"Word on the street is a trainee broke his back last night on the rocks. True?" Pastor Wayne asked.

Pete and Josh exchanged looks. "Yes, sir," Josh said.

"What happened?"

"Everyone worries about the dangerous evolution on those boulders south of the Del. You have to time it just right, or else," Josh said. "One of the boats timed it wrong, and a team-mate got injured."

"Is he okay?" Pastor Wayne asked. "Darlin and I have been praying."

Pete stared at the sky.

"He could move his limbs this morning," Josh said.

"You guys are nuts."

"Yes, sir."

"I don't really have a need to know," Pastor Wayne said. "But will you guys be around much this summer? Darlin wants Pete to sing for the services, a solo."

Pete rubbed his chin. "Have her send me the dates."

"Great. See you Saturday night."

They nuked an enchilada casserole Amy had sent home with Josh the night before and flipped on a baseball game while they ate. "Tell Amy thanks," Pete said as he cut a large wedge of apple pie and plopped ice cream on top.

Once done, they both went to bed. Pete for the night, Josh until the alarm went off at nine thirty.

Wearing an SDSU T-shirt and flannel pajama bottoms, Amy yawned when she let him into the house around ten. She pointed to the green canvas bag over his shoulder. "What are you up to?"

"No good. Where's my accomplice?" He smelled popcorn.

"Waiting in the family room with movies lined up. She thought you'd like *Raiders of the Lost Ark*."

"One of my favorites." Josh headed to the patio, where he left his bag. Mrs. Martin, wearing a red velour tracksuit, greeted him when he joined her. "Start the movie."

Amy fell asleep on the couch before Indiana Jones even reached Nepal. Mrs. Martin pointed to an afghan and Josh covered the sleeping woman with care. She looked so pretty, sleeping with her capable hands tucked next to her cheek. He paused.

"Go ahead and kiss her," Mrs. Martin said. "This movie doesn't have enough romance for me."

Josh grinned. "Maybe later."

They skipped the second movie and once past the Boy Scout opening scene in *Indiana Jones and the Last Crusade*, Josh slipped outside to check on events. He tapped a message into his phone and then put on the wet suit he'd brought in his duffel bag.

"How soon?" Mrs. Martin asked. He noted a pair of heavy binoculars on the end table.

"About half an hour. They're faster this year." He applied green and black camo paint to his face.

"Do you need the war paint?" Mrs. Martin asked.

"It never hurts to practice. I'm not supposed to be out there."

Josh slung his waterproof bag over his shoulder and gave Mrs. Martin a hand up. Amy stirred and opened her eyes. Of course she screamed.

"Go to bed, dear," Mrs. Martin said. "You're obviously not ready for commando activity yet."

Josh felt madcap. "I'll carry you to bed if you like."

Amy sat up and ran her fingers through her hair. "What are you doing?"

"Clandestine operation, lady, and I got to go. See you." He offered Mrs. Martin the crook of his arm and escorted her outside.

Hell Week usually took place during the dark phase of the moon, and often during poor weather to make life even more miserable for prospective SEALs. When Josh had swum out before to meet the crews on their "around the world" paddle from the NAB docks on the bay side to BUD/S's Pacific Ocean beachfront, he'd often swum in the rain. On this beautiful, warm July night, with the San Diego city lights gleaming across the water, tonight's angel delivery looked easy.

He nestled Mrs. Martin into a deck chair he'd set at the water's edge, and put on his flippers and mask. Amy, mercifully quiet, retrieved a chair of her own. Josh could hear splashing activity coming from the southeast, and once he had the lead boat in sight, he slid into the water.

By Thursday night of Hell Week, the BUD/S trainees had been awake some ninety hours and reeled with fatigue. The fast pace of the operation meant even though they stuffed their faces at all four meals, including midrats—middle of the night rations—they were always hungry. Some SEALs had mercy on the trainees and secretly provided encouragement and food. Pete had gone into the water off the Del the night before to pass out candy bars to boats of trainees offshore, for example. Tonight was Josh's turn.

With seven boats headed his way, Josh had seven double ziplock bags full of high energy candy and granola bars. He just had to get to the trainees and toss in the encouragement.

Josh didn't have to swim far offshore to meet the first black rubber inflatable boat with six focused paddlers throwing up spray. As always, they were startled when he intercepted them by grabbing the inflated rubber side of the boat.

"Hey," cried a trainee.

"God bless you." Josh tossed in the stuffed bag and ducked underwater.

The second and third boats were paddling hard to keep up with the first and trickier to catch, but Josh managed to lob in his bags and shout his encouragement before swimming away. BUD/S instructors rode in a small boat not far off and he didn't want to be seen.

The men in boat four were leaning over the side to retrieve a man overboard. One of their teammates had fallen asleep while paddling, and they were hauling him back in. Josh could not interfere with the operation, but as soon as they got themselves squared away, he tossed in a bag and blessing.

Boat five team members sang a pirate song to keep up their morale and yelled "Arg." Boat six barely moved, the men so bleary with exhaustion. Those six men grabbed the bag with enthusiasm and the leader gave Josh a thumbs-up. He had one bag of provisions left in his sack. Where was the last boat?

Josh looked to the southeast toward the bridge. The instructor boat hung back, so he knew another group must be coming, but from the water he couldn't see anything. Josh glanced at Mrs. Martin's waterfront, now a considerable distance away. He knew she had binoculars, but would she be watching him?

Amy wore a white robe and was pointing past him. Treading water, he finally saw the boat coming, but very slowly. Only two paddlers. Very odd. He looked toward the instructor boat. They had binoculars aimed in the same direction.

Josh had to be careful not to get caught. He went under the water, deep, and swam as fast as he could.

He came up about ten yards off the boat's port side and saw activity in the back of the six-man boat. Josh heard the frantic cursing of frightened, tired men. He tossed in the bag. "What's up?"

The starboard paddler shrieked. "Man down."

Josh glanced toward the instructor boat. "What happened?"

"Body flailing like a chicken dancing. We don't know what's wrong with him."

"Signal the instructors. Is he breathing? I'm a medic, but I can't help you," Josh said. He hated situations like this.

"We can't signal the instructors. We got to finish."

Josh heard wet, slurry coughing. "Is he coughing up blood? You need help."

The inflatable boat lurched. Several men muttered, "No."

The men were exhausted, wet, and scared. He knew that. Josh wasn't supposed to be there. He knew that. If the instructors came over, several trainees would probably quit. He knew they didn't want to do that. But one of their men didn't sound good, and they were freaking out.

"Three of you paddle," Josh shouted. "Two of you huddle up to the man to get him warm. You need to call the instructors. I'm out of here." Even as he stroked toward shore, Josh prayed. He saw the instructor boat zoom over to the inflatable, and then he went underwater and disappeared into the night like a good angel.

He swam silently up to shore where Mrs. Martin's clear voice carried over the water. "There's a price to pay when you love someone with a difficult job. You ask yourself, do I love him enough to let him be the person God created him to be? My High was a fighter and a man of convictions. Your Josh is the same."

"My Josh?" Amy said.

"I've seen the way you two look at each other. He's a good man. Don't let your fear get in the way of loving him."

Josh treaded water to hear her response.

"I don't see him through the binoculars," Amy finally said. "Do you suppose he's okay?"

Mrs. Martin laughed. "He's trained to be silent and stealthy. Josh is probably closer than you think."

"I can't face him. Good night." Josh heard her dash away.

He pulled himself out of the water and slipped off his flippers and mask.

"Did I get you the information you wanted?" Mrs. Martin asked.

Water poured off him, and he looked toward the house. "I'm not sure."

"She'll be back when she realizes she didn't help me to my room."

Josh kissed Mrs. Martin on the cheek. "I think I'll let her sleep on it."

He saluted the admiral's wife, grabbed his green bag, and slipped off into the night.

Amy played Celtic lullabies on the CD in the massage room. She'd found candles that smelled of baby powder and lit them. When she adjusted the pillows under the pregnant woman's enlarged belly, the woman cooed. Amy loved doing massage on expectant mothers.

Sophie moved her own hands protectively around the front part of her belly while Amy slipped another pillow beneath it. "I feel like I'm surrounded by marshmallows."

"As long as you're relaxed." Amy started with soft, long strokes up the woman's right leg, which was on top. "Do you know if you're having a boy or a girl?"

Sophie prattled about the little girl due in two months. This massage was an anniversary gift from her husband, currently deployed. "We've been married five years today, and I haven't known where he was half the time. The only anniversary we celebrated together was the first one."

"Sounds difficult," Amy murmured. "Will he be here for the birth?"

"I don't know. I never know."

"How do you handle it?" Amy moved to the woman's feet. She had to be careful not to handle pressure points in the legs, but pregnant women loved having their feet massaged.

"I'm thankful for the good times when he's home. The other wives and girlfriends help, and my job keeps me busy. Life will change with the baby, but another wife is due about the same time, and we're good friends." Sophie yawned.

Amy focused on the woman's toes. Pregnancy often slowed circulation in the feet.

Another yawn. "Fortunately Brad doesn't bring the job home with him. When he's here, he's all mine."

Amy remembered how scary Josh looked three weeks ago when he'd swum out to meet the BUD/S trainees. In his black wet suit with the paint on his face, he looked capable of anything and dangerous in a not-so-good way. "Do you ever see him in his battle gear?"

"Sure. A man in uniform is so exciting, don't you think? What service is your guy in?"

Sophie's right hip bothered her, so Amy kneaded the area carefully. "SEALs. Except he's not really my guy, but maybe…"

He'd been surprisingly cheerful since that night he launched into the water from Mrs. Martin's house, almost too kind. She'd caught him watching her as they worked on the lessening-of-fear project, and the look on his face made her blush. She had no idea what he thought half the time, and it both drew her to him and made her squirm.

"They're all so mysterious. You can never be sure if they're committed to you until they demonstrate their reliability." The woman giggled. "That's the opposite of demonstrated unreliability. If you meet a guy who acts unreliable, run away."

Demonstrated unreliability. Amy turned the phrase over in her mind as she pushed through knots with her fingers. Josh had used the term in derision when describing guys he didn't like: unacceptable, losers.

Amy knew. The biggest horror of her life was her father's demonstration of how unreliable he was all those years ago on the bridge. She glanced at the red numbers on the clock. It was time to tell Josh the truth about the bridge.

He had demonstrated his reliability, stopping by four nights a week to take her to the bridge and work with her fear. Josh now could drive her across without much panic on her part, though she wasn't sure the butterflies would ever go away.

She needed to tell him the truth. Josh had demonstrated his right to know.

Amy picked up Sophie's hand and ran it along her belly.

"Here's your baby's spine, she's head down. Perfect." The baby rolled and shoved back with her foot. Moments like these were another reason why Amy loved her job.

Amy pushed out the double glass doors of the spa at six fifteen. A gull cried offshore and she shielded her eyes to look toward the beach. She saw families dragging gear home, sunbathers packing up as the air cooled, and navy joggers. On Wednesdays, Josh usually came up from the NAB compound via the ocean side. As she took the short path to the beach, she glanced up at the Sun Deck Bar and Grill. Was a thin white-blond man looking in her direction?

She didn't want to know.

Sandpipers cut across the hard sand when she reached the water line. The waves rolled in gently that afternoon. On such a clear day, she could make out Point Cabrillo's lighthouse on the other side of the bay entrance. A cell phone ding brought a message: See you soon. Need to make a call.

Amy shut her eyes. The clean ocean air felt good after eight hours in the sweet-smelling but closed-in spa. Tonight she would be honest and tell Josh the sources of her fears.

"I finally caught up with you," said a reedy thin voice over her head.

Amy opened her eyes. Ethan.

"Haven't you been getting my messages? I've left word nearly every day with the staff."

She could feel the old fear rising, just like when she approached the bridge. But after all these weeks of desensitization, Amy recognized the symptoms and knew she could deal with it. How many times had Josh told her to confront her fears?

Ethan represented the other worry. Amy took a deep breath.

Another text came: You know the guy?

She tapped back: I need to deal with him. Fear.

Need help?

She glanced at the glowering Ethan. Not yet.

Okay. Got your back.

Amy smiled. He did indeed have her back. As she closed her phone, she saw Josh twenty feet down the beach.

What was the first step he had taught her about dealing with fear? Define your situation.

"Are you a guest here at the Del, Ethan?" she asked.

Ethan shrugged. "I've been coming by for a drink all week. Yeah."

"Are you actually staying at the hotel?"

Ethan grinned. "Is this a pitch for me to get a room? Sure. I'll get a room if you'll join me."

Josh's advice: "Expect the unexpected."

Del training: "Be polite."

Bible verse: "Love your enemies."

Amy shook her head. "No, thank you."

Ethan shifted in the sand. "I've been trying to book a massage with you. They won't do it. If I get a room and book an in-room massage, would you come up and make me feel better?"

It would be so easy to tell him she had a SEAL boyfriend who would beat him up for suggesting such a thing, but Amy knew she needed to deal with Ethan on her own terms. Josh had moved within earshot, and his face had gone blank. Uncharacteristically, however, he flexed his hands. Did he really have her back?

Amy smiled.

Ethan sucked in his breath. "You will? I'll do it."

She tucked the tendrils of her hair behind her ear and gentled her voice. "Don't bother, Ethan. I can't help you for several reasons. It's against policy. I don't do in-room massages, and, frankly, I don't want to."

Out of the corner of her eye, she caught Josh's nod.

"I thought you liked me," Ethan whined.

"Why did you think that?"

Error. Do not engage the fear. Deal with it and move on. Her stomach fluttered.

"You shared your notes. You ate lunch with me before class. You were happy to see me. I protected you from those jocks." His arms flailed like a giant albatross.

A text: Don't engage. Focus.

Amy snapped her phone shut and brought in her elbows close to her body. She paused and thought. This foolish guy was not her enemy. He could not hurt her. She needed to take control.

She looked up at him and saw how he tried to use his height to intimidate. But he was a hollow man of no substance. If she puffed, he'd blow away. Amy took a deep breath.

"To me, you're a classroom acquaintance from San Diego State. I lent you notes because you said you had a personal need. I found out you lied to me. I'm sorry if you misunderstood a friendly person's well-meant help, but that's all it was. I don't want to see you again."

He grabbed her left elbow. Amy stood her ground. "Take your hand off me."

Ethan leaned toward her, his arm tightening. "It's not so easy, honey."

The sneer in his voice brought up another memory, and nausea sprang into Amy's throat. The urge to strike Ethan made her raise her arm, but Josh's words from several days ago slipped through her brain. *"Use your head. Don't let your worries about the future overcome your present circumstances."*

Ethan wasn't shaking her arm hard. She had time to clear her head. Ethan was a straw man, weak in mind, soul, and body. Amy's strong right hand plucked his hand off her arm and she stepped away.

She held up her phone. "If you touch me again, I'll call the police. This is the last time you will contact me. I don't want to know you and I have no idea why you think you're interested in me. We have next to no past and no future. Besides, I have a boyfriend."

"What boyfriend?"

Her hero stepped right up. "I'm Josh Murphy. Who are you?"

The contrast couldn't have been more obvious: Ethan an adolescent wisp of straw, and Josh a strong, confident man. Warmth and pride filled Amy's heart.

"You should have told me." Ethan stalked away muttering obscenities.

"Would you have listened?" Amy murmured.

Josh watched Ethan kick sand as he tramped back to the Del. "Nice job, Amy. But you should have told me about him."

She shook her head. "There was nothing to tell. Thanks for stepping into the role of boyfriend."

He touched the tip of her nose. "It was easy."

Chapter 23

Thursdays were long days for Josh. After PT, he accompanied Flip to therapy in San Diego, and then had to catch up on his regular work when they got back. It took several hours out of the day twice a week to help his teammate, but they both had learned a lot.

He didn't participate in the personal counseling Flip received, but he took a turn with the goggles and the desensitization training. Josh now felt better about small spaces himself, especially after he and Flip climbed into a cardboard tube mock-up of the same tight spot that had triggered claustrophobic reactions in both of them. Flip managed it, and they'd visit a sub at Point Loma soon to try it for real.

Going into a missile tower on the sub would be the final test. Josh knew he could handle it.

Josh had shared the coping skills with Amy and watched her confidence bloom as they worked on her bridge phobia. He was proud of how yesterday she had taken all the techniques and applied them to her previously unmentioned fear of men. That made several things more understandable about her, though Josh still shook his head over her trust in him the first night he drove her over the bridge.

What was he going to do about Amy? Josh asked himself for the thousandth time as he approached Mrs. Martin's gate. If that jerk on the beach had tried one more thing, if Amy hadn't waved him off, Josh would have killed the guy. Right there in front of the Hotel Del with innocent women and children building sand castles around him.

He hadn't had to confess such a sin of hatred since the day Jed died all those years ago.

But he'd confessed it and let it go. Tonight Amy had something to tell him. What could it possibly be?

Josh stood on the sidewalk looking at the bell. What did he want to say to her? What did he dare tell her? What was she to him, anyway?

A caring, beautiful, hard-working young woman who shared his values and lit up when she saw him.

He knew that.

Soft and warm with inviting eyes and a bewitching smile. She could even cook and apparently gave a terrific massage.

He loved her.

Yes, he did.

But his military career was too hard for a woman. Maybe he should turn away and not come back to save Amy some heartache.

"Are you coming in?" Amy's sweet voice came over the speaker box. "I buzzed open the gate."

He'd better hear what she had to say first.

If nothing more, surely she deserved to be kissed good-bye.

Even if it was dangerous.

"Are you hungry?" Amy asked when he walked into the house.

"I ate before I came. You ready to take on the bridge again? After you stood up to that guy yesterday, it should be a piece of cake."

"I had my breakthrough yesterday. I'm not worried about the bridge anymore."

Josh narrowed his eyes. "I don't think so. You look a little nervous to me."

"Let's go outside. Mrs. Martin is reading in her room, and I need to talk to you."

He followed her out, noting, as always, her trim figure and smooth movements. She led him down to the water. San Diego's skyline sprawled across the bay, lights twinkling on and off as night fell. He noted the view, but kept his eyes on the young woman who stared at her twisting hands. A brackish, almost brine scent came from the water splashing against the quay.

"Would it help if we prayed?" he asked. What could the issue be?

"Always. Lord, please give me strength to talk to Josh and help him understand."

He waited. She finally met his eyes.

"You asked me once if I remembered what made me afraid of bridges. I didn't want to think about it."

Josh shrugged. "You said you didn't remember."

She swallowed. "I didn't tell you the truth. The height has always bothered me and the thought of all the air underneath, but I never intellectually worried the bridge would collapse."

"Good. It's not going to."

"I know. It's more psychological."

Josh shook his head. "I saw your very big physical reaction to riding over the bridge."

"I know, but as I've thought and prayed about what bothered me about the bridge, I had to face what I really was afraid of."

"And…"

"My parents had a very rocky marriage with lots of fighting and arguing, sometimes physical violence. My mom didn't handle my father well. Late one night when I was five, we crossed the suspension bridge to Long Beach to pick him up."

Josh watched her. He wasn't surprised to hear her fear had an emotional component. After all the time he'd spent with the therapists and Flip, he understood many issues played into a phobia as strong as Amy's. "Go on."

"Dad took the wheel of the car and we drove off. My parents started quarreling. I tried to calm him by rubbing his shoulder, but he yelled and struck at me. Mom intervened, they screamed at each other and it went on and on. Then we reached the bridge. He drove erratically, and I thought he'd go over the side. Maybe Mom did, too, because she grabbed the wheel. He pushed her away and when we got to the top, Dad stopped the car and got out."

"Was there any traffic?" Josh asked.

Amy sighed and looked toward the city. A ferry jaunted across the water with a high toot. She caught her hair up into two hands and twisted it out of her face. He could smell a sweet flower scent and had to battle an impulse to reach for her.

"No. It was late at night, foggy, dark, and lonely on top of a high bridge. Mom got out of the car and tried to talk to him. He shouted, 'If you don't want me anymore, I don't want you.' Mom got behind the wheel and drove away crying. My dad never came home again."

"Whoa. I'm sorry."

She whispered. "For a long time we thought he had jumped, but eventually he wrote. My mother never drove over the bridge again, and neither did I."

Now he did reach for her. "What happened to him?"

"I didn't see him again for eleven years. I've only seen him a handful of times since."

He rubbed her back, and his hand trembled at the heat. "Have you made your peace with him?"

She spoke into his shoulder, which also felt on fire. "What

I told you yesterday about being afraid of men had to do with my dad abandoning me on the bridge. But as we've worked on fear these last weeks, I felt stronger, more able to face men who treated me wrong. That's what happened with Ethan. I saw how weak he is, and I wasn't afraid anymore. I wrote my dad a letter last night and mailed it today."

He brushed her hair back, but he couldn't see her face. "What did you say?"

"I told him what happened that night on the bridge terrified me, and that I never considered how hard things were for him. I described how you've shown me one man can be trusted. Because of you, I've conquered my fear of men and bridges." She took a deep breath. "With you at my back, I don't have to be afraid anymore."

All Josh could think of was how much he wanted to kiss her again. He needed to stay clearheaded. "I'm glad you wrote your dad. That was a brave and big step toward healing the relationship. I'm thankful if I played a role, but it's God who's been at work in your heart and your mind."

Amy nodded. "All the prayers and practice have made me more confident. I told Dad I forgave him and the last bit of fear lifted. I'm cured."

"Why do you think you're cured?"

"I used all our techniques yesterday with Ethan. I'm not afraid anymore. Didn't I demonstrate it?"

Josh cleared his throat. "Listen, Amy, recovering from phobias is not always simple, and you're mixing two fears together. Let's see if you can drive across the bridge before you pronounce yourself cured. It will only take half an hour. Let's go now."

"Not tonight, I don't want to go anywhere. We'll go tomorrow after Bible study."

"Tomorrow night for sure." Josh paused, but as a corpsman felt obligated to continue. "I don't want to discourage you, but some people need more than what we've done to overcome phobias. Flip sees a professional therapist. I've been doing research, but I'm not a trained counselor. Your reaction to the bridge was huge."

She made a face. "But I'm not anywhere near as nervous as I used to be."

"You've done beautifully, babe, but I don't want your hard work undone if you're not ready. Maybe you should see a counselor to make sure."

She stepped away and narrowed her eyes. "You don't think I'm cured?"

"The final step is to go into the real life situation carefully monitored and see how you do. Flip and I are going to the Point Loma sub base tomorrow. We'll put on our gear and go inside a missile silo. That's not exactly what caused all the problems but it's close enough."

"Are you afraid of the silo?" Amy asked.

As night fell, sounds magnified across the water. The rhythmic thrum of an engine sounded as a backdrop. Josh thought of the sub base across the bay.

He crossed his arms. "I'd like you to pray for me. I've been uneasy with enclosed spaces ever since I got back to San Diego. Not terrified like you on the bridge, but not calm. I think Chief is testing me, too."

"What happens if you fail the test?"

Josh swallowed. "Best case, I go to virtual therapy myself. Worst case, I can't be a SEAL anymore."

Amy gazed at him a long time. "I guess we'll cross that bridge when you come to it. I'll pray."

Then she slipped her arms around his neck and kissed him.

Josh couldn't believe the house didn't catch on fire.

Amy was scarcely out of bed Friday morning when her boss Kathy called and asked her to swap days off with another therapist.

Amy checked her schedule. "Sure." She clicked off the

phone, pleased. A surprise day off meant she could catch up on life. Amy turned on her laptop. She had a college registration pass soon, and she needed to figure out her schedule for the fall semester. For the first time she had enough money for tuition before school started next month. What a great summer.

She joined Mrs. Martin and a surprise guest, Darlin, on the patio for lunch. "You probably didn't know we've been prayer buddies for years," Darlin said.

"I would have prayed with you if I'd known you were here," Amy said. "Josh is doing something dangerous today and asked me to pray."

The two older women exchanged a look, and Darlin reached for her hand with a jingle of her bracelets. "Let's pray right now. You pray since you know the issue."

Amy took the offered hand slowly. "Why do you look concerned?"

Darlin's eyes were kind. "Anytime a SEAL asks for prayer, we need to pray. They've got a dangerous job."

Amy shut her eyes. "Lord, please be with Josh and Flip today on the submarine. Keep them calm, and if fear rises up, help them deal with it effectively. Protect them and restore Flip to full confidence. Thanks for what You've done with my fears and keep them safe. Amen."

Mrs. Martin's caregiver had prepared an exquisite shrimp salad served with warm yeasty-smelling wheat rolls. "I love to come here because everything tastes good and I don't have to make it." Darlin laughed.

"You earn your lunch with your prayers," Mrs. Martin said.

"How do you know so much about SEALs?" Amy asked.

Darlin toyed with a crouton. "Living on Coronado, you pick up information. We know Josh and Pete and a couple others. I've had SEAL wives in my Bible study over the years. It's a difficult life and takes a special person. I pray for them often."

"But they're just people," Amy said. "It irritates me how Josh tries to scare me off. He's always telling me the life is too hard, as if I can't measure up. I don't like it."

"He's making sure you're counting the costs," Darlin said. "SEALs remind me of the Francine Rivers novel, *The Last Sin Eater*. Somebody has to do the dirty work for society, the hard jobs no one else wants. SEALs do those jobs to keep our country safe. They pay a high price for their level of commitment."

"Joshua is a fine young man. But all navy sailors are," Mrs. Martin said.

"Wayne worries about them," Darlin continued. "We've seen too many SEAL relationships fall apart with the stress of the job. Maybe he's trying to protect your heart as well as his own."

Amy tried to hide her smile. "His heart?"

Darlin pushed the bracelets up on her arm. "He's been in a protective stance ever since he met you. That first day, he asked us if we knew of a place on the island where you could stay. We've seen the way he looks at you. You know his intentions are right."

Amy nodded and glowed inside.

"Do not break his heart," Mrs. Martin said. "I'm on his side. I always root for the navy guy in a romance."

"Yes, ma'am." Amy felt giddy with joy. "I think he's testing me, to make sure I've got what it takes to be with him."

"What will it take?" Darlin asked.

"I've just got to drive across the bridge. I'll show him tonight."

Darlin laughed. "You go, girl!"

Amy picked up her glass of iced tea, and they clicked their glasses together. "I'll show him."

Chapter 24

Josh didn't like submarines. The odor of ripe men, smoke, old food, and diesel oil always made him wrinkle his nose when he stood above a sub hatch. Who wanted to go into a submarine when you could stand outside in the fresh air and sunshine on a typical gorgeous San Diego day?

When the therapists from the virtual therapy center joined them, Flip and Josh slung the heavy green canvas bags containing all their diving gear over their shoulders and grabbed the ladder to climb down the hatch. Chief and their SEAL platoon commander, Lieutenant Cable, were with them, too.

"You guys are lucky this boat pulled in for a port call. They're headed back to Washington tomorrow, so make it a good exercise," Chief said.

"Have you ever been in one of these silos before, Chief?" Josh asked. "You're welcome to join us."

"I'll be staying dry watching you on video," Chief said.

The USS Ohio's commanding officer met them at the bottom of the ladder, shook hands, and introduced them to the chief of the boat, or COB, who would control the evolution. They followed the COB through the control room, down stairs, past the mess deck to the area midship where the Trident ballistic missiles were once housed.

The boat had been modified so the launch tubes could accommodate SEALs and their equipment. Flip and Josh would enter one of the SEAL lock-out chambers with a regular navy diver. All three would wear their scuba gear and wait while the perpendicular tube was flooded with water. The submarine had plenty of monitoring equipment, and the controlled evolution could be stopped if things went bad. This would be the final test to see if Flip had conquered his claustrophobia.

And maybe mine, too, Josh thought.

"A simple test," the therapist explained. "This tube is eighty-seven inches in diameter and large enough for six SEALs wearing full gear. The space is comparable to what you had trouble with in the Gulf. We'll seal the door shut and watch how you do over the video monitors. If you're feeling fine after ten minutes, give us a thumbs-up and we'll fill the tube with water."

Josh set the timer on his waterproof watch and climbed through the hatch in the side of the tube. Air regulators lined the interior of the tube, which had a ladder going up to the top of the submarine, forty-four feet above. It was dry inside, but the COB and his crew would fill it with water if Flip could handle it.

Flip and the diver off the sub followed him. Before they closed the hatch, Chief leaned in. "Hey, Doc, no heroics. If you guys can't handle it, let us know."

"Aye-aye," Josh said.

The door slammed shut and the three men stood together in the bottom of the former missile silo. The diver killed time by pointing out features, and Josh watched Flip.

Blank face.

Not good.

"Let's put our face masks down," Josh said. "We're supposed to duplicate the Gulf experience."

Flip adjusted his mask into place, and Josh did the same. He lost his ability to watch Flip's face clearly, but this was similar to the Gulf. Three minutes passed. "You okay?"

"Yep."

"What kind of mission were you guys on?" the diver asked.

Josh didn't want to talk. "Classified."

"Right. Sorry."

Flip turned to him. "Can you give me a little space?"

"Sure." Josh grabbed on to the metal ladder and inserted his right fin into the bottom rung. He stepped up and then climbed several more rungs until he was five feet above Flip. "This any better?"

Flip nodded.

Josh checked his watch. Eight minutes. He yawned. He wasn't having any problems, but then only three men were in the silo. Chief and the lieutenant should have joined them. Josh said as much into the air.

No answer.

"Can they hear us?" Josh asked the diver.

"Yes and see us. Time's up. You okay? I'll tell them to flood the silo."

Josh looked at his teammate. "How are you feeling, Flip?"

"I'm okay." Flip rubbed his thumb against his index finger and stared straight ahead. Josh wasn't so sure.

"Listen, Flip, we took this opportunity because the sub is here. If you need more time with the virtual therapy center, you've got it. We don't need to flood the tube if you need more time."

"I said I'm okay," Flip shouted. He put up his thumb. "Fill 'er up, Chief."

Water sprayed in from jets near Flip's and the diver's feet, knees, and shoulders. From his perch on the ladder with his right elbow hooked to keep him in place, Josh watched with interest as the tube flooded. Water quickly covered the tops of their flippers. It rose to their ankles. It burbled past their calves.

Josh leaned down. "You okay, Flip?"

The diver shook his head. "I don't think he is."

Josh removed his face mask. "Take off your mask, Flip. I need to see your face."

Flip bobbed his head, slowly at first and then faster.

"Chief, turn off the water," Josh yelled.

The diver hit buttons on the wall.

Shaking started, and then a convulsion ran through Flip's body. Josh needed to get to him.

Flip ripped off his mask, flung back his head and howled. Josh jumped to reach him in the knee-deep water.

And that's the last he remembered.

"I need to get moving," Darlin said as she polished off the last spoonful of lemon sorbet. "A delightful meal, but I've got to practice the organ. I'll see you tonight, Amy."

Her phone rang as she walked out the door. Darlin waved good-bye and took the call while Amy watched. Darlin gasped and whirled around, her eyes wide. "Yes, she's right here. Of course we'll pray. Thanks."

"What's wrong?" Amy asked.

"Pete called Wayne. There's been an accident. They took Josh to Balboa with a serious injury."

Mrs. Martin joined her in the doorway, leaning on her cane. "What happened?"

"He didn't know. He said Josh was knocked unconscious. He wanted me to tell Amy to pray."

"How bad?" Amy's heart pounded and she felt breathless.

"I don't know."

"Let's find out," Mrs. Martin said. "Get your purse, Amy. We'll go in my car."

"I can drive," Amy said, trying not to imagine what could

have gone wrong. "They were in a submarine. They were testing them for claustrophobia."

Mrs. Martin pushed the button opening the garage door and hobbled toward the garage. "Drive my car. I'm an admiral's wife. Rank has its privileges."

"Do you want me to come, too?" Darlin asked.

"Amy and I will handle this. Call others to pray." Mrs. Martin climbed into her snub-nosed late-model Cadillac. She pointed to the two white stars on the windshield. "In this car, we can park anywhere."

Amy had never driven the car before, and Mrs. Martin had to explain how to put it in gear. She turned around in the driveway, hit the electric gate opener, and drove onto First Avenue, mercifully empty that afternoon.

She drove down the street, taking the right onto Orange Avenue and stopped in the left hand turn lane onto Fourth Street. "What could have happened to Josh? Did the claustrophobia overcome him?"

Mrs. Martin didn't think so. "I'm sure it was an accident. He's too smart to fall apart."

"He's certainly been working with Flip on it," Amy said. The light turned green and she made the turn, gunning the powerful engine. As they came over the rise, she could see the Coronado Bridge ahead. She couldn't think of it. She had to focus on Josh. "Dear God, please take care of him."

"Amen," Mrs. Martin said.

The car sped down the street past houses and then the green trees at the edge of Tidelands Park. They flashed under the abandoned tollbooth canopy and by the last-chance U-turn spot, and then up the bridge.

"His chief would not put him into any dangerous situations," Mrs. Martin said. "It's in the navy's best interest to keep her men safe."

"I don't understand why Josh got hurt," Amy said, focusing on the two-lane road. A utility truck rumbled by. "He was worried about Flip."

"Perhaps he tried to save Flip, and Flip attacked him," Mrs. Martin suggested.

Amy noted small blue squares attached to the light poles. "What do those signs say?"

Her passenger waved her hand. "Nothing important. Probably has to do with road maintenance."

No clouds cluttered the sky; no wind blew. All Amy could see was the ribbon of gray road and the blue sky overhead. She swallowed, but kept driving.

"I imagine they'll take him to the emergency room, don't you think?" Mrs. Martin said.

"Unless he's in surgery. I should have gotten Pete's phone number. How will we find out?"

"No problem at all. We'll go to the front desk. I'll ask for the commanding officer, and he'll help us. He's an old friend of Susan's."

Amy couldn't believe her ears. "The commanding officer? I don't think so. Unless it's really bad, why should we bother the commanding officer?"

"Don't borrow trouble." Mrs. Martin's voice cut in sharply. "We'll find out when we get there. I'm sure Pete will be happy to make sure you get to Joshua's side as quickly as possible."

Amy glanced at her. "But I'm not married to him. The navy may not let me see him. He may not even want to see me."

Mrs. Martin smiled, her red lipstick glowing against her clear skin and porcelain white hair. "I believe he's going to want to see you very much."

"I don't know how you can be so sure," Amy said. She glanced at the speedometer. Eighty miles per hour. She tapped the brakes.

"Because, my dear." Mrs. Martin's voice trembled. "You've just driven over the Coronado Bridge."

They were down, and the I-5 interchange loomed. Petco

Park faced them on the left, and the freeway interchange spun into different directions. Amy snatched a look into the rearview mirror and saw the curling span of the bridge receding.

Her mouth dropped open, and then she grinned. She'd told Josh she could do it. But would she be able to tell him she had done it? Amy pushed down the gas pedal again.

Mrs. Martin was correct. The Cadillac with two stars could park in front of the hospital. They didn't have to go to the front desk, however, because they saw Pete pacing in front of the hospital. He waved and helped Mrs. Martin out of the car.

"How is he? What happened?" Amy demanded.

Pete stopped. "How did you get here?"

"Love conquers the bridge," Mrs. Martin said. "She drove right over."

His smile lit up his face. "Wow. Congratulations. Josh will be excited."

"How is he? What happened?" she asked again.

Pete shook his head. "He fell off a ladder, banged his head, and then had to be hauled out of the submarine in a weird gurney arrangement. He's got a broken leg and a concussion and will be in the hospital a couple days, but he'll be okay."

"So it wasn't claustrophobia?" Amy asked.

Pete stood tall. "What do you know about that?"

"He asked me to pray."

Pete stared off into the distance. "No. Just his leg. Flip we're not sure about, but Josh is okay." He looked down at her and smiled again. "And with you here, he'll be more than okay. Let's see what's up."

"What happened to you?" Amy asked.

"I must be hallucinating," Josh said. "I can't believe you're here, and Josie, too. When did Pete get you?"

Pete laughed. "Tell him, Amy."

"I had to make sure you were okay. I was praying for you,"

Amy said. She looked at Mrs. Martin sitting in the chair beside the bed. The admiral's wife winked.

"Thanks." Josh grimaced. "We were in the missile tube. I hit my head and broke my leg. That's all I know."

He looked pale under his sun-browned skin, but his blue eyes shone. A thick white bandage crossed his forehead. Tubes and electrical monitoring wires spiraled out of his checked cotton hospital gown, and his heavily bandaged leg was elevated under the blanket. The blood pressure cuff started up with a sigh, lights blinked across monitors, and the whole room reeked of antiseptic.

"I had to see you with my own eyes," Amy said. "Nothing could stop me from finding out how you were."

"Amy jumped right in the car," Mrs. Martin said. "I came along to find out how you were myself."

"Other than my leg, I'm fine." He grinned. "More than fine, seeing Amy."

"No problems in the sub?" Amy asked.

"None. How about you?"

"I'm triumphant. I conquered the bridge."

"Thanks for bringing them over, Pete."

Pete barked a laugh. "Don't look at me. I've been here with you."

Josh's eyes widened. A slow grin started as he gazed at Amy. "Did you drive?"

"Yes!" She felt almost dizzy at Josh's stunned expression.

He licked his lips and finally spoke. "I guess this means you're brave enough to be my girl."

Would he always have the ability to rile her?

"I just drove over the Coronado Bridge to see you," Amy said, leaning closer. "Is that the best you can do?"

Josh disentangled one of his hands from the plastic tethering him to the bed. "You've got what it takes, Amy. I think you've always been a capable, strong woman. I was just afraid to tell you so."

Amy took his free hand and rubbed circles with her fingers. "What does that mean?"

"I'm afraid I fell in love with you in spite of myself."

Amy smiled. "That's one of the few things I wasn't afraid of. I love you, Josh."

He reached for her as she leaned down, meeting halfway in a fearless kiss that lit up the room.

"Don't you love it when the sailor gets the girl?" Mrs. Martin said.

Pete laughed. "My favorite ending is when the SEAL meets his match, and they live happily ever after."

* * * * *

REQUEST YOUR FREE BOOKS!

2 FREE CHRISTIAN NOVELS
PLUS 2
FREE
MYSTERY GIFTS

HEARTSONG
PRESENTS

REQUEST YOUR FREE BOOKS!

2 FREE INSPIRATIONAL NOVELS
PLUS 2
FREE
MYSTERY GIFTS

Love Inspired

YES! Please send me 2 FREE Love Inspired® novels and my 2 FREE mystery gifts (gifts are worth about $10). After receiving them, if I don't wish to receive any more books, I can return the shipping statement marked "cancel." If I don't cancel, I will receive 6 brand-new novels every month and be billed just $4.49 per book in the U.S. or $4.99 per book in Canada. That's a savings of at least 22% off the cover price. It's quite a bargain! Shipping and handling is just 50¢ per book in the U.S. and 75¢ per book in Canada.* I understand that accepting the 2 free books and gifts places me under no obligation to buy anything. I can always return a shipment and cancel at any time. Even if I never buy another book, the two free books and gifts are mine to keep forever.   105/305 IDN FVYV

Name _____ (PLEASE PRINT) _____

Address _____ Apt. #

City _____ State/Prov. _____ Zip/Postal Code

Signature (if under 18, a parent or guardian must sign)

Mail to the Harlequin® Reader Service:
IN U.S.A.: P.O. Box 1867, Buffalo, NY 14240-1867
IN CANADA: P.O. Box 609, Fort Erie, Ontario L2A 5X3

**Are you a subscriber to Love Inspired books
and want to receive the larger-print edition?
Call 1-800-873-8635 or visit www.ReaderService.com.**

* Terms and prices subject to change without notice. Prices do not include applicable taxes. Sales tax applicable in N.Y. Canadian residents will be charged applicable taxes. Offer not valid in Quebec. This offer is limited to one order per household. Not valid for current subscribers to Love Inspired books. All orders subject to credit approval. Credit or debit balances in a customer's account(s) may be offset by any other outstanding balance owed by or to the customer. Please allow 4 to 6 weeks for delivery. Offer available while quantities last.

Your Privacy—The Harlequin® Reader Service is committed to protecting your privacy. Our Privacy Policy is available online at www.ReaderService.com or upon request from the Harlequin Reader Service.
We make a portion of our mailing list available to reputable third parties that offer products we believe may interest you. If you prefer that we not exchange your name with third parties, or if you wish to clarify or modify your communication preferences, please visit us at www.ReaderService.com/consumerchoice or write to us at Harlequin Reader Service Preference Service, P.O. Box 9062, Buffalo, NY 14269. Include your complete name and address.

LIDIR13

ReaderService.com

Manage your account online!

- Review your order history
- Manage your payments
- Update your address

> ### We've designed the Harlequin® Reader Service website just for you.

Enjoy all the features!

- Reader excerpts from any series
- Respond to mailings and special monthly offers
- Discover new series available to you
- Browse the Bonus Bucks catalog
- Share your feedback

Visit us at:
ReaderService.com

RS13

HEARTSONG
PRESENTS

Look out for 4 new
Heartsong Presents books next month!

**Every month 4 inspiring faith-filled
romances will be available in stores.**

These contemporary and historical Christian
romances emphasize God's role in every
relationship and reinforce the importance of
faith, hope and love.

Love Inspired

To Trust or Not to Trust a Cowboy?

Former Dallas detective Jackson Stroud was set on moving
to a new town for his dream job, until he makes a pit stop
and discovers on the doorstep of a café an abandoned
newborn and Shelby Grace, a waitress looking for a fresh
start. He decides to help Shelby find the baby's mother,
and through their quest he believes he's finally found a
place to belong, while Shelby's convinced he will move on
eventually. What will it take to convince Shelby that this is
one cowboy she can count on?

Bundle of Joy
by
Annie Jones

Available March 2013!

www.LoveInspiredBooks.com

LI87801

Matchmaker—Matched!

For Ellie O'Brien, finding the perfect partner is easy—as long as it's for the other people in the town of Peppin, Texas. When her handsome childhood friend Lawson Williams jokingly proposes, the town returns the favor and decides a romance is in order for them. But when secrets in both their pasts threaten their future, can the efforts of an entire town be enough to help them claim a love as big and bold as Texas itself?

A TEXAS-MADE MATCH

by **Noelle Marchand**

Available in March wherever books are sold.

www.LoveInspiredBooks.com

LIH82957